Behind
Blue Eyes

Behind

Blue Eyes

Book Two
The Last Werewolf Hunter

by

William Woodall

Jeremiah Press · *Antoine, Arkansas*

Jeremiah Press
PO Box 3
Antoine, AR 71922

Cover image dhruvchandra, used by permission.

First published by Jeremiah Press on 09/22/2010.

Printed in the United States of America.

This book is printed on acid-free paper.

ISBN 978-0-9819641-7-1

Library of Congress Control Number: 2010913763

For Cameron

All things work together for good to those who love God,
To those who are the called according to His purpose.

- Romans 8:28

Thoughts of a Werewolf Hunter
By Zachary James Trewick

"If you pour light into the darkness for love of the light, then you'll never lack for a reward."

"You never feel so afraid as when you're alone, and if somebody who loves you will just stand beside you when the hard time comes, then it makes all the difference in the world."

"I couldn't go inside the store soaking wet and with no shoes on, unfortunately. They kinda frown on that, even in Arkansas."

"At the heart of darkness, there's always a nugget of gold."

"I was full of doubts, and it was downright terrifying to think about trusting an old promise that much, even one from God. I was ashamed of myself for thinking like that, but I won't pretend I didn't. All I can say is that sometimes the world seems very real and the stuff you learn in church seems very faint and far away."

"Sometimes we even laugh, but it's the kind of laughter that can live with sorrow at its heart. Maybe that's the best kind."

"I'm always reminded that nothing is too hard and no enemy is too terrible for God, and that we conquer through Love, or not at all."

"Sometimes people do things like that and it catches you off guard how much they love you. I wish it wasn't so hard to remember it all the time."

"When you've been blessed, you don't hold the gift in your hands and try to keep it for yourself. If you do that, it turns to poison before long."

"It's dishonest to willingly shut your eyes and choose to be ignorant when you don't have to be."

"Hope will sneak up and bite you on the foot when you least expect it, if you don't watch yourself."

"Justin always says you can't ever expect God to do the same thing twice. That all of eternity isn't enough for Him to express Himself even once, and that you shouldn't be sorry for that, but instead look forward to whatever good thing He has in store next."

Contents

Chapter One

They caught me on a night when the moon was full, just like I always knew they would.

It was late September, and if you took a deep breath you could catch the first taste of fall in the air. I love that time of year, and that's why I went down to the lake that night to toss pebbles in the water and watch the ripples wash the shore. Justin and Eileen were at a conference in Houston, so I had the whole place to myself for the weekend.

Maybe I should have known better than to go traipsing down there alone on a full moon night, but it had been a long time since I ran away from home, almost two years in fact, and I guess I was starting to get careless. Besides that, I wasn't expecting anything to happen right there in my own back yard.

Not till the dude grabbed me, anyway.

Without a snarl or a growl, or even so much as a crunch of dead leaves under his feet to give me any warning, somebody snatched me from behind and slapped his hairy paw across my mouth to keep me from yelling.

Oh, I fought like a tiger on crack, but it didn't do me any good. I had one arm free and I used it to yank loose the silver cross I always wore around my neck for just such an emergency. It was made with a sharp point at each end, and as soon as I got hold of it I swung my hand up and nailed the dude right on the forearm. You might not think it sounds like much of a weapon, but for me a sharp piece of silver was better than all the guns and knives in the world.

The man cursed, and I think he almost let go of me for a second. I felt his hold loosen up just a little bit, but not quite enough for me to break free. Instead I felt a sharp little prickle in my side where his other arm was wrapped around me, right under my ribs. At first I thought it was a knife, but then I found out later it was a shot of horse tranquilizer.

I had time to be surprised that the silver hadn't done anything to the man, and I remember wondering what went wrong. Then everything went black.

* * * * * * *

I woke up with a pounding headache inside a dark stuffy place that smelled like wet dirt. I wasn't thinking too clearly yet, and the first thing that crossed my mind was that I was inside a coffin. That was such a horrible idea that I screamed, or at least I tried to. That's when I found out my mouth was covered with duct tape.

My hands and feet were taped up, too, and that's an awfully scary way to wake up, if you've never tried it. For a little while, terror threatened to drown out everything.

I took a deep breath and forced myself to calm down, though. I might be packed like a sardine in a can, but I was still alive and I didn't seem to be hurt except for the headache. My hands were taped together at the wrists, but I could still move my arms. I reached up and felt the ceiling, which was no more than a foot above my face. It felt like cardboard, and there was enough give that I could tell it wasn't a coffin at least. Not that I've ever actually been inside a coffin before, you know, but I was willing to bet they didn't make them out of cardboard. Nobody is *that* cheap and tacky.

That did wonders for my nerves, and I started to explore the situation a little better. The first step to getting yourself out of a pinch is to find out exactly what you're up against.

Whoever taped me up must have been in a hurry, because they were awfully careless about it. If they'd thought to tape my arms down to my sides then I probably would have been out of luck, but as it was I had some wiggle room. I brought my hands up to my face and pulled the tape off my mouth first, and then I started gnawing on the strip around my wrists.

Duct tape glue is really nasty, just in case you ever wondered. I wouldn't advise chewing on it unless you absolutely have to. It gets stuck in between your teeth and I think they must flavor it with dirty motor oil, the way it tastes. I felt like gagging.

It took me a good long time to chew my hands free. The tape tore hair off my wrists when I pulled it loose and I gritted my teeth from the pain. I didn't dare make noise, though, so I had to pull slowly even though it made it hurt more.

As soon as I could, I felt in my right jeans pocket where my cell phone should be. It was still there, so I flipped it open and used the backlight from the screen to look around. I was definitely inside a cardboard box, just like I thought; one that was barely big enough to hold me. There was some half-dried red clay mud on the walls down close to my feet, which must have been where the wet dirt smell had been coming from.

I tried to call Justin or Eileen, but all I got was a "call failed" message. Wherever I was, there was no cell service. I didn't waste time crying over it, though; I just closed the phone and slipped it back in my pocket. I didn't want to run the battery down when I might need it later.

As it turned out, I still had my pocketknife and my billfold and all my other stuff, too. The only thing missing was the silver cross from around my neck, and I might have dropped that on the ground when the man knocked me out. I felt almost naked without it.

I strained my ears to hear the slightest noise, but it was quieter than a cave in there. No engine or traffic sounds, no machinery, no voices, nothing.

I finally decided it was stupid to wait around for the man with the hairy hands to come back and find me. I had to get out of that box.

I pushed up with my palms, but the lid would only move a little bit before it stopped firmly. It was probably taped shut on the outside or some such thing, but I was ready for that.

I opened the little blade on my knife and stuck it into the side of the box way up high, and then sliced down in one smooth cut. You should never let your knife get dull, you know. You can never be sure when you might need it. You might never get trapped inside a cardboard box, but then again you never know. Just a few hours ago I never would have seen it coming myself. I always sharpened both blades at least once a week, and right then I was glad I did. I made two more quick cuts and then knocked out a piece of cardboard about twelve inches square.

The first thing I saw when I got the hole open was a spare tire lying flat on some dirty gray carpet, and the back of a leather car seat. I couldn't see much more than that because of the angle.

There was darned little room to move around inside that box, and I had to struggle a while and nearly scraped an ear off on the edge of the hole, but eventually I was able to push my head out to get a better look around. I was in the back cargo hold of a Bronco or a Blazer or something like that. The box I was in was tied up with plastic cords, just like I thought. Good enough.

I quickly sliced another cut in the box to make the hole bigger, and then wormed the rest of my body out.

The windows were tinted really dark, but it was daylight outside and I could see well enough. There wasn't much out there except a dirt road lined with thick pine trees behind me, and in front there was what looked like a deer camp. There were five or six cinder block buildings of pretty good size, and two other cars parked not far away. I was close enough to the nearest building to see dew still glistening and steaming on the metal roof, so it couldn't be very late yet. There was nobody in sight, but I knew better than to hang around. Somebody might show up any second.

I checked real quick to make sure there were no keys in the car. I knew that was probably too much to expect, but you never know. People are careless sometimes.

Oh, I don't really have my license yet, by the way, but I do know how to drive when I need to. Justin lets me drive the truck now and then on back roads where there's no traffic. I'd never tried to drive anything alone yet, but I figured this was an emergency and nobody would blame me for doing whatever I had to do.

No keys, though, so I gave up on the idea of driving away. Instead, I eased open the back hatch of the Blazer just enough to slither out, and then shut it again as quiet as a whisper. If I had to walk then that's what I'd do.

I was barefooted and that complicated things, but I knew I couldn't stay on the road. That was the first place they'd look when they found me gone. I wasn't thrilled with the idea of walking through the briers and rocks with no shoes on, but it looked like I didn't have much choice. So I took a deep breath and trotted off into the woods as fast as my feet could take me.

I didn't think anybody had seen me, but of course I couldn't be sure. For the next hour or so I didn't slow down for a second, even though I never heard anybody coming after me. I knew enough to head straight toward the sun so I wouldn't start walking in circles. I didn't want to run around all day and then end up right back at the camp again. Following the sun would keep me going in a straight line, at least. But as for where in the world I was, that was a whole 'nother question.

I checked now and then to see if my phone had service yet, but it never did.

The land was really steep and rocky in places, and that slowed me down. You can't climb as fast as you can walk, and the rocks were hard on my bare feet, just like I knew they would be.

After a while I came to a rocky stream, and I stopped to wash my sweaty face and take a drink. It looked like it was going to be another bull-roaster kind of day. September is like that now and then; it can still be hotter than a hen in a wool sweater, some days. I couldn't help wishing this hadn't been one of those times, but there was nothing I could do about it. In the meantime the creek was clear and cold, and the water tasted delicious to a boy who was almost dying of thirst by then. I splashed some of it on the back of my neck and my arms, and then I sat down on a big gray boulder and dangled my sore feet in the current. It felt so good I didn't want to get up.

But I knew I wasn't out of danger yet, and I didn't dare just sit and wait for Hairy Paws to come scoop me up. If he was a good enough tracker or if he had dogs then he could probably still follow my trail through the woods and catch me. I wasn't sure about that, and when you don't know then you don't take chances.

The little creek flowed somewhere off to the south, and I decided to follow it for a while. If you're lost in the woods, that's almost always a good idea. A flowing stream will usually lead you to people sooner or later. It also keeps you from getting lost and gives you water to drink, and you don't leave any trail or any scent to follow.

Daddy taught me all those things, back when we still used to talk about stuff sometimes, and for just a second I was grateful to him for that. Then I remembered he probably only did it to make me a better werewolf someday, and that wrecked the whole thing and left a sour taste in my mouth and for a while I almost hated him.

Justin would have told me to let it go and love him for whatever good there was in him, but that's hard, you know. It's easy to get bitter when somebody does you so much wrong, and every time I thought I was over it, little things like that kept reminding me at the weirdest times.

I decided not to think about it right then.

I slogged down the creek for several hours, and watched it get gradually bigger. The land was awfully mountainous, and I'm not sure how I could ever have made my way through if I hadn't had the stream. There were lots of little waterfalls about three or four feet high, but I could jump over those if I was careful. It was hot work doing all that hiking, and those occasional dunks kept me cool. I was hungry enough to gnaw the bark off the trees, but there was nothing I could do about that.

After a while, I came to a bridge.

Well, sort of. It was just a little foot bridge that crossed over the creek, and there were some picnic tables and a sidewalk on the left bank. It looked like a little park or some such thing, but there wasn't a soul to be seen.

Somebody had mowed the grass around the picnic tables not more than two or three days ago, and there was a Styrofoam cup still sitting on one of them, still half full of somebody's old coffee. When I nosed around a bit more I found a parking area, and then a dirt road that led away from it.

For a while I couldn't make up my mind whether to take a chance on the road or to keep following the creek a little farther downstream. The coffee cup and the mowed grass made me think this was a place where people visited fairly often, so after a lot of thinking I decided maybe the road would be a better choice.

Before I left the campground or park or whatever it was, I scrounged an empty plastic Coke bottle from the trash can and rinsed it out several times before filling it up at the creek. I knew I'd get thirsty and there was no telling the next time I'd come across any water.

It wasn't all that long before the road came to a T-junction, and there was a sign posted. The left arrow said Hwy 8 - 5 miles, and the right arrow said something about a lake. I don't remember exactly, because as soon as I saw that highway sign I didn't care what might be in the other direction. I turned left.

The sign forgot to mention that the road ran steeply uphill most of the way, but I can promise you I noticed. It took me about three or four hours, but eventually I did make it to the highway with no particular trouble, except for my feet. They were killing me by then from walking barefoot on those gravel roads. They eat up your skin like sandpaper.

When I got to the highway there was no sign to tell me which way to go, so I shrugged and went east. It kept the sun out of my face, and I figured that was as good a reason as any.

I felt pretty good about things at that point. It seemed like the worst was behind me. I was tired and hungry and uncomfortable in other ways, but that was okay. I could probably thumb a ride to the nearest town, and then I could call Justin and have him come get me. And in the meantime while I waited for him to get there, I still had nineteen dollars in my pocket. I was looking forward to a nice juicy cheeseburger. It's amazing how delicious food is when you haven't eaten in a while.

So I stuck out my thumb whenever I heard a car coming, and waited for somebody to pick me up. Hitchhiking is kind of a chancy business, you know. You can never be sure who might stop, and there are some very strange people in the world to say the least. But right then I was ready to make friends with just about anybody.

That highway might have been built on the moon for all the cars I saw, but no matter how far out in the woods it is, every road has at least a little traffic. Two or three cars blew right past me without stopping, which is about what I expected. But after a while, a green Mustang with Alabama plates pulled over not far in front of me.

I hobbled up as fast as I could on my sore feet, and opened the door and sat down. The air conditioner was running, and the cold air inside felt wonderful. It was a girl driving, which sort of surprised me. Girls don't usually stop for anybody, but maybe she thought I was young enough to be harmless.

"You look like you could use a ride," she said with a smile.

"Yeah, I just need to get to the nearest store," I told her.

"Sure thing," she agreed. She had long blonde hair and she couldn't possibly have been more than twenty. I laid my head back on the seat and pretended to close my eyes since I didn't really want to talk, but she was so pretty I couldn't help watching her out of the slit of my left eye. She reminded me of someone I might have seen before, but I couldn't think who or where. It niggled at my mind like a gnat, till I finally decided it wasn't important.

A few miles down the road we went around a sharp curve, and she put both hands on the steering wheel to turn it. That's when I noticed what long, beautiful fingernails she had. Long, beautiful, *sharp* fingernails, perfectly manicured. Almost like claws, in fact. That's when I knew her for what she was.

My heart almost stopped, and I'm sure it came right up in my throat. I swear I could feel it sitting there on the back of my tongue. I don't think I could have said a word if my life depended on it.

I didn't let on. I kept pretending to rest while I thought desperately of how to get myself out of the hole I'd stepped into.

It was just barely possible that she didn't know who I was or have anything to do with me, of course. I knew how unlikely that was even while I was thinking it, but hope will make you grasp at straws and make a fool out of you if you're not careful. I knew I'd be crazy to believe she had nothing to do with me. That was way too much of a coincidence.

On the other hand, I was fairly sure she didn't realize (yet) that I knew she was a werewolf, and that gave me one slim advantage. She wouldn't be on her guard quite so much.

On the third hand, if she was specifically looking for me, there was no way she'd really take me to a store and drop me off, or even let me out of the car. Not unless I did some really smooth talking between now and then. I got a firm handle on my voice (I hoped) and opened my eyes with a fake yawn.

"So what's a pretty girl like you doing out here in the middle of nowhere?" I asked her with a smile. Eileen always tells me what a cute boy I am and what beautiful blue eyes I have, and I always used to laugh it off when she said such things, but if there was any chance it could help me then I was willing to give it a shot. Girls like all that flirty stuff for some reason, and I was betting this one was no different. She laughed a little.

"Oh, I'm just here with my family on vacation. Mom sent me to the store to get some ice and things," she said. It sounded reasonable, even though I didn't believe it for a second.

"You're from Alabama?" I asked.

"Yeah, Huntsville. Guess you saw my tags, huh?" she asked.

"Yeah, I did. Uh, so you're just going to the nearest store, then?" I asked, like I didn't care much.

"Yeah, but that's in Glenwood. The store in Norman doesn't have Cherry Dr. Pepper, and Mom won't drink anything else," she said glibly. I pounced on that.

"Would you mind very much if I rode to Glenwood with you? I know it's a lot to ask, but I'd really appreciate it," I said. I had to play things real carefully so I didn't make her suspicious. I wanted her to think she had me fooled. She probably wouldn't attack me as long as I wasn't putting up a struggle. It was a lot easier for her if I went along willingly as long as possible. The gloves would only come off when I tried to get away from her.

"Sure, I guess," she shrugged, "it's only a few extra miles."

"Thanks a lot. It's not every day you run into a girl as awesome as you," I told her, and smiled my best smile again. I was in danger of overdoing it, but all I can say is that I wasn't at my best at the time. Sitting next to somebody who could rip you to shreds with her bare hands makes it hard to think straight, believe it or not. The girl didn't seem to notice, though. She just laughed again.

"Yeah, that's what my boyfriend tells me all the time," she said. That's what I was expecting her to say, so I had that one covered.

"Well, dang. Lucky guy," I said, snapping my fingers. She smiled.

"Thanks anyway, honey. It was a sweet thing to say," she told me. I was pretty sure I had her fooled at that point, so I didn't push it any more.

Not long after that, we started passing a few houses and things, and it didn't look quite so deserted as it did before. We came to a junction and turned right, and I saw a gas station up ahead a few blocks. That's what I'd been waiting for, and it was time to make it or break it. I crossed my fingers and prayed for it to work.

Chapter Two

"Hey, could we make a pit stop at that gas station for just a second? I'm starving," I asked her. She didn't look really happy with that idea, but as long as we were still playing the game it was hard for her to say no. She tried, though.

"Do you think it could wait till we get to Glenwood?" she asked reluctantly.

"Well, see. . . if I don't eat then I get car sick really bad. I promise it won't take but a minute," I squeaked, doing my best to look as sick as possible. That almost always works, and this girl was no exception. Her eyes opened wide and she pulled over in front of the gas station right away. Nobody likes to get vomit in their car.

I opened the car door and walked into the station, which had a hole in the wall convenience store on one side. As soon as I was sure the girl couldn't see me, I took out my cell phone and tried to call Justin again, only to find that I still didn't have any service. I texted him instead just on the off chance that he might get it later.

I bought a Coke and some Cool Ranch Doritos since I really *was* dying of hunger, and when I paid for them I brought up the subject with the clerk.

"Uh, can I use the phone, ma'am? It's really important," I asked her.

"Is it a local call?" she asked. I knew that was coming.

"No, but I'm willing to pay for it. I'll give you five bucks," I said, pulling out the cash. The sight of money has a wonderful way of motivating people sometimes.

"Well, you can use mine if you want to, but keep it short if you can," she told me, handing me her cell phone. I noticed she used a different company than mine, but that was okay. That was probably why she had service and I didn't. I called Justin as fast as I could push the buttons.

All I got was his voicemail, but that didn't surprise me much. He was still at that dadgummed conference, and he'd probably be in and out of seminars where he couldn't get to his phone all day long. I left him a message saying I was at a gas station in Norman, Arkansas, and asked him to come get me. I couldn't say much more than that, not with the clerk standing right there in front of me. She'd think I was loony. I figured Justin was smart enough to fill in the blanks well enough, anyway. He'd know if I asked him to come all the way from Houston to pick me up, there'd have to be a really good reason for it. I told him to hurry as fast as he could and I'd call him back later when I had a chance to. Then I gave the girl back her phone and the five dollars.

I got one other thing while I was there, too. They had a rack of souvenir items against the wall, and amongst the postcards and shot glasses and assorted trinkets, I found something better than I dared hope for: a set of red heart-shaped ear rings with a ceramic bass in the center. I guess they were supposed to mean *"I love bass fishing"* or something like that. They were perfect!

No, I do *not* wear them, but the reason I wanted them was because they had sterling silver posts. It said so, right there on the label. They were $8.95 and that just about cleaned me out, but it was well worth it. Now I had a powerful weapon to use.

There was a garage attached to the store where they changed tires and things like that, so I went that way and walked out the back of the building so the girl in the car wouldn't see me leave. I'm pretty sure I wasn't supposed to use the back door, but nobody said anything.

As soon as I got outside I hurried away, being sure to keep the gas station between me and the Mustang for as long as I could. While I walked I tore the ear rings open and dropped the extra one in my pocket while I held the other one in my hand. I wanted to be ready to defend myself if I had to.

I quickly found out there aren't too many places to hide in Norman, and I started to get a little scared again. I didn't dare stay out in the open for too long. Before very much longer Blondie would figure out I'd slipped the noose, and then she'd be after me. She'd probably be furious, too, and there'd be no fooling her next time if she caught me again.

I spied a bridge over a little river and made a beeline for that, walking as fast as I could without running. If you start to run then people get curious, and I didn't want anybody to remember seeing me.

I made it to the bridge in double quick time, and ducked underneath it after glancing around to make sure nobody was watching. There were a lot of big gray rocks under there and a little bit of sandy beach down next to the water, so it wasn't too bad of a place to hole up for a while. I climbed way up near the top where it was harder for anybody to see me, and there I sat.

I tore into the chips and the coke while I had time, and I don't think anything ever tasted so good.

Hiding under a bridge like a troll in a fairy tale was not the best plan in the world, I have to admit, but it was the only thing I could think of right then.

Now and then I heard cars passing by on the bridge over my head. They made the whole bridge shake and rattle around me like it was about to fall apart any second, but none of them stopped. The girl in the green car must have figured out I'd flown the coop by then, and I was willing to bet she was hot on my heels. Others too, most likely. Back up on the roads was the last place on earth I needed to be.

I moved downhill a little bit so the bridge didn't make so much noise when cars went by, and then I sat there tossing pebbles into the water for a while and thinking about what I should do. The river was clear and blue, gurgling and splashing over gravel bars and rocks, but it was no more than about waist deep. It was hot even in the shade, and the water looked inviting to say the least. I wished it was just an ordinary day and I could jump in for a swim.

I noticed an old river tube caught in the debris under the bridge stanchions, and that gave me an idea. There was *one* way I could get far away without being seen on the roads, if I could make it work.

I picked my way down to the bank, then waded out there to look at the tube a little closer. Sure enough, it had a hole in it about the size of a pencil, but it seemed otherwise okay. A holey tube won't do you much good for long, but it might work just long enough to save my bacon, if I played my cards right.

I stuck my left thumb in the hole to plug it, then started to blow up the tube with my mouth. I left it a little bit loose and flabby on purpose so there would be less chance of leaking, and waited a minute to see whether it held air. It seemed to be holding steady for the moment at least, and I decided to risk it. If it blew out on me later, I could always swim if I had to.

The water was shallow enough that I could climb into the tube without too much trouble, so I clumsily got into the seat while trying to leave my thumb plugging the hole. It wasn't easy to twist myself around and find a comfortable spot, but I finally managed it. Then I paddled out into the current as best I could with one hand. Before long the stream grabbed me, and away I went at a pretty good clip.

Floating a river is fun, if you've never tried it. I'd done it lots of times with Justin and Eileen. Not usually in a leaky tube, to be sure, but as long as it held air I was okay with it. The late afternoon sun sparkled off the water, which was just a tad bit chilly but not too cold to handle. If it had been very much later in the year I wouldn't have been able to stand it, but as it was I didn't mind so much.

I wrapped up my phone in the empty Doritos bag from the gas station, rolling it up as tight as I could to keep it from getting wet. I could brush the chip crumbs off later, but phones don't handle water too well.

I thought I knew where I was, now. I'd been to Norman once before to go digging for quartz crystals and to float this very river for a few miles. At least I thought it was the same river. It had been a year or so ago, but the more I thought about it the more certain I was. I was maybe a hundred miles or so from home. I just needed to head south, and that's the way the river would take me anyway for now.

The Caddo River doesn't really have what you'd call whitewater, exactly. Just a few little riffles and such, not enough to even pay attention to. I remembered that much. I'd been in a canoe the last time I was here, but it shouldn't make much difference. I had to keep an eye out for logs and rocks and willow strainers, and that's about it. With a bit of luck, it would carry me all the way to Glenwood.

I'd have to get out of the water there and start watching my back again. The river didn't go much farther before it fed into Lake Degray, and then there wouldn't be any current to carry me anymore. So, Glenwood it would have to be.

Blondie probably didn't have a clue where I was right that minute, but she might very well guess where I was headed, especially since it was the only close town. She surely knew where I lived, and she probably also knew there was no other way for me to get there except by going through Glenwood. Not without going forty or fifty miles out of the way, and I didn't have time or money for that. There were mountains all around, and the river and the highway followed the one and only gap through them. She'd be watching that place like a hawk on a mouse-hole.

But for the meantime I was safe from prying eyes, so I relaxed and laid my head back on the tube and closed my eyes. I knew better than to go to sleep, but I wanted to think.

Who were these people that seemed so bent on catching me, and what did they want? I knew the girl was a werewolf; her fingernails gave that away, and it was hard for me to believe she wasn't connected with the people at the deer camp. But on the other hand, why hadn't my silver cross done anything to the man who caught me in my own back yard? That made me wonder if maybe he *wasn't* one. But if not, then why was he helping them? And again, what did they want with me?

That's the one thing I kept coming back to. Why me? And why now? I had wolves in my family, sure, but I hadn't seen or talked to them in two years. No one had ever bothered Justin just because his sister was a *loup-garou,* so why should it matter if my parents were? What did they want?

Try as I might, there was no way I could figure that one out. Not unless I found out more, and I didn't know any way of doing that right now.

The river gurgled and whispered to itself, and the quiet and the solitude were starting to make me sleepy. I raised my head to shake loose the cobwebs; it would never do to fall asleep in the tube and then hit a log or a rock and get dumped in the river with no warning a split second after waking up. That was a good way to lose my tube in the current or even drown.

The rest of the afternoon passed without too much to say about it. The banks glided by smoothly and swiftly, and the occasional riffle was no trouble. Every now and then I had to blow some more air into the tube when it got too flabby. I almost got tangled up in a willow strainer once, at a place where the current passed close to the bank and tried to pull me right under a thicket of low-hanging branches. I had to paddle hard with my right hand to keep from getting sucked in there.

After a few hours I passed a place where the bank had been turned into a parking lot, and I felt the water turn suddenly warm around me right through there, which startled me. I guess there was a hot spring under the water or some such thing. It felt nice, but after I passed through it and got back into the ordinary water it only reminded me how cold I was. I thought again about how it was really too late in the year to be floating like this.

There were some people lounging around on the tailgate of a red pickup truck in the parking lot, and they seemed to think it was way too cold to be out there on the river, too.

"You're gonna freeze your butt off, boy!" they called out cheerfully. They meant well, so I didn't take offense.

"Nah, I'm all good!" I yelled back, just as cheerfully. They laughed and waved me off. I didn't mind the conversation so much, but what did make me uneasy was that I could see the highway the whole time I was in that little area. Anybody driving by could have seen me on the river just by turning their head.

That didn't happen, though, and it wasn't more than a few minutes till I floated under another bridge and back into the woods again. It only seemed like a week.

By that time I was getting really tired of riding on that dadgummed tube, and dusk was coming on pretty fast, too. It wouldn't be more than thirty minutes till the stars came out. Any other time I wouldn't have even thought about staying out on the river after dark, and certainly not without at least the moon. It was way too dangerous.

But as it was, I was probably safer on the water than I was on the road. The moon would be up in an hour or so, and as long as I kept my eyes peeled and my ears pricked and paid attention to what was around me, it would probably be okay.

I hoped.

And so it was. I won't say I enjoyed it much, but I've gone through worse things. After a long time I saw another big highway bridge up ahead and a bunch of yellow and red canoes down below it on the left bank. There was a shallow gravel bar where I ran aground on purpose, and then I clambered my way out of the river like a waterlogged rat. I was shivering by then and being wet didn't help, but there wasn't much I could do about it.

I climbed up the bank and came to the highway, then scooted across an old football field till I got to a Wright's grocery store. I couldn't go inside soaking wet and with no shoes on, unfortunately. They kinda frown on that, even in Arkansas.

Instead, I went behind the store beside the trash dumpster and took off my shirt and wrung as much water out of it as I could, and then I did the same thing with my shorts. It felt weird getting buck naked in a public place like that, I have to say. It was fairly dark behind the store, but still. If anybody had come waltzing around the corner right then I think I would have died three times before I could hit the concrete.

I was still damp after I finished, but at least I was dry enough not to drip river water all over the place. There was nothing I could do about my bare feet, so I decided I'd just have to brazen it out. Maybe they wouldn't say anything to me about it if I didn't draw attention to myself.

So I breezed inside like I owned the place and got me a turkey and cheese sandwich and paid for it with almost the last of my change. That one bag of chips hadn't done much for me, and even that was hours and hours ago. Nobody said anything about my feet.

I went back outside and ate my food, and that's when I found out my cell phone was soaked. The water must have got in at some point, in spite of the Doritos bag. I shouldn't have been surprised, I don't guess. I sighed and wiped it as dry as I could on my shirt tail. There was a chance it might work again after it dried out. Sometimes they do.

There was a pay phone in front of the grocery store, and I still had fifty cents left in my pocket. I walked over there and tried to call Justin one more time. All I got was his voicemail again, but I let him know I was in Glenwood at the grocery store and he needed to come get me as soon as he could. I told him everything this time, since there was nobody around to hear what I was saying.

That's when I got careless. Instead of finding somewhere to hole up and hide for a while, like I should have done, I went back and sat down on the bench in front of the grocery store. I don't know what I was thinking, looking back. Maybe somewhere in the back of my mind I had the notion that Justin might try to call the payphone back or something like that. I don't know what I thought, honestly. But I was bone tired, and I felt safe at that point, and so I stupidly sat there in a public place in full view of the highway. I could kick myself for it, but there you go.

After a while, a dark blue Blazer pulled into the parking lot, and I paid no attention even when it circled slowly around the lot and came near the front of the store. Sometimes people do that, you know, when they're looking for a parking spot close to the doors. I think they probably waste more time circling the lot than they would if they just walked all the way.

Anyway it was late and so this one found a spot pretty close to the front, and three or four people got out. It was too dark for me to see them very well or I might have thought one of them looked awfully familiar, but as it was I didn't notice.

One of them pulled something out of her purse, and a second later I felt a sharp sting when something hit me in the chest. I just barely had time to look down and see a dart sticking out of my shirt, and after that everything went dark.

Chapter Three

I guess they carried me all the way back to the deer camp after they knocked me out, because when I woke up that's where I was again. Only this time I wasn't taped up in a cardboard box that I could cut my way out of. I was lying on a creaky old metal hospital bed, with my left wrist handcuffed to the bed frame.

"That's right; you won't get away so easy this time, you slippery little fish," the blonde girl from the car told me. She was standing at the foot of my bed, and there wasn't a trace of a smile on her lips now. She was probably right about that, I thought to myself, but I wasn't going to give her the satisfaction of seeing that I was afraid.

"Where am I?" I demanded, giving her the nastiest scowl I could manage. She did smile then, and it wasn't a very nice smile either.

"I don't see why I should tell you anything, Zach," she said. Somehow I wasn't surprised she knew my name, but I let it pass. She was trying to score points, and I wasn't going to play that silly little game with her.

"Fine, then. Don't tell me anything," I said calmly. I knew they wanted something from me, and that meant they'd have to tell me what it was sooner or later. All I had to do was wait, and she'd have to spill the beans whether she wanted to or not.

I could tell my answer annoyed her, but that was good. People will sometimes say things they didn't mean to say if you can get them riled up.

"The question you ought to be asking is *why* you're here, and there's no secret about that one. You're here to join us, and this time there won't be any last minute escapes," she said sweetly. I didn't have to ask her what she meant by that. I knew only too well.

That news rattled me a bit in spite of myself, and I couldn't resist asking her a question.

"But why? I already told everybody I didn't want anything to do with that stuff. I won't make trouble for anybody, I just want to be left alone," I told her.

"'Fraid it doesn't work that way, honey. Not for *you*, anyway," she added as an afterthought. That made me want to ask her what was so dadgummed special about *me,* but I saved that for later. When you're talking to an enemy you should never let them know what you're really interested in. It gives them the upper hand. I learned that from reading *The Prince* last year in English class. All that political intrigue and stuff bored me to tears at the time, but right now my tongue was the only weapon I had, so I figured I better make it count.

"You can't make me if I don't want to; I know how it works," I said, changing the subject.

"Maybe not, but if you ever want to leave here and go home then you'll agree. Otherwise. . . " she shrugged.

"You can't keep me here forever," I said.

"We can keep you as long as we need to, honey, and that's all that matters," she said, with another one of those hateful smiles.

Deep down, I was seriously afraid she might be right about that. Out in the middle of nowhere like this, who would there be to help me? Nobody, that's who. Justin thought I was in

Glenwood, and what would he do when he got there and I was gone? I was sure he'd look for me, but it was the longest of long shots that he'd ever find me in a place like this. He wouldn't even be able to call the police to help. All they'd do would be to call my parents. Fat lot of good *that* would do me.

I thought about all that in the space of a few seconds, and I soon decided the only thing I could do right then was pretend to go along with it for a while. They wouldn't trust me, of course, but they might let their guard down enough to give me a chance to escape again. If I was sullen and resentful then that would never happen.

I changed my tack.

"So you're telling me if I agree to this, then you'll leave me alone and let me go home?" I asked.

"Sure, if that's what you want. But you won't, Zach. Not after you become one of us. I can promise you that," she told me confidently.

Now came the difficult part, so I picked my words carefully.

"Well. . . I *might* do it if it means I never have to deal with yall's ugly faces anymore, but there's something I want first," I finally told her. She frowned a little bit.

"You don't have a lot of room to ask for much, Zach," she said. Then she seemed to think better of it.

"But if it will get you to do this willingly, and if it's not too unreasonable, then we might be able to make a deal. What do you want?" she asked me.

That was just the opportunity I'd been waiting for. I didn't really want anything from them, of course; I was just playing for time. But I couldn't ask for something stupid or that would blow the whole thing. It had to be something they could believe I might really want, and hopefully something only they could give me. It couldn't be anything too easy or it wouldn't gain me any time, and it couldn't be too hard or they'd refuse. That sounds like a tall order, I know, but I thought I had the perfect thing in mind.

"I want to see my sister first," I told her. I could tell that wasn't something Blondie was expecting to hear, but she was good at hiding her surprise.

"I see," she finally said, half to herself. She thought about it for a while longer, seeming to chew it over in her mind.

Then she looked at me for a long time, like she was trying to decide if I was for real or not. Maybe it helped that in my heart of hearts I really did want to see Lola; I don't know. Whatever the reason, Blondie seemed like she made up her mind to go along with it, at least for the time being.

"I'll have to see about that before I give you an answer," she finally said. That was about what I thought she'd say, so I just nodded.

"In the meantime I'll let you loose for a little bit, but you better not try anything. There's no way out of this room except through the door, and you certainly won't get out that way. I suggest you be good this time. If we're going to start trusting each other then it needs to go both ways," she told me.

I tried to look very solemn and serious at that, but inside I was overjoyed. I didn't even crack a smile, though. If I did then she might not turn me loose.

She pulled a key from her pocket and unlatched the handcuffs that held me to the bed, then slipped them in her pocket along with the key. I sat up, rubbing my wrist where the metal had chafed it.

"See, we can be nice to each other instead of having to do things the hard way, can't we?" she asked.

I think I liked her less and less the more she talked, so I didn't say anything to that. I can't stand people who look down their noses at everybody and think they're so high and mighty, and Blondie seemed like exactly that kind of person.

She didn't wait for an answer, thankfully; just knocked on the door to have somebody on the other side let her out. I heard the snick of a heavy-duty lock when the door shut behind her.

As soon as her footsteps faded away down the hall, I jumped up and started to explore the room to see if there was any way out. I had no intention of waiting to see what her answer was about Lola. If I found a way to bust out of there, I meant to take it. I knew what they wanted now, and the worst they could do was catch me and lock me up again. I wouldn't be much worse off than I already was.

It didn't take me very long to eyeball the whole place, and I have to say things didn't look too good. The walls were plain cinder block, painted over with three or four layers of off-white paint, and the only windows were some narrow slits too high up on the walls to even see out of. I think a cat would have had a hard time squeezing through one of them. There was a rusty steel door that led into a bathroom, which had the same cinderblock walls and slitted windows as the main room.

For furniture there was nothing but the old metal hospital bed that looked like it came from a salvage yard. There were no sheets on the mattress, no pillow, and just a plain wool blanket to cover up with. The rest of the room was totally empty.

The floors were concrete, partly covered by some brown and white tiles that had come loose in places. The door that led outside into the hall was a big monster of a thing, metal except for a diamond-shaped window about the size of my palm. Just big enough for them to be able to look in and see what I was doing whenever they felt like it. There was no keyhole on my side of the door.

I sat down on the bed again and thought about it a while. I wasn't ready to give up just yet, but I was blessed if I could think of a way to get out of there.

Sometimes when you go stale on a problem, it helps to think about something else for a while. I might not be able to figure a way out of there just yet, but I could still chew on some other things I didn't have the answers to. Like why the wolves wanted me so bad, for one thing. There was something about me in particular that had their knickers in a knot, something which didn't apply to Justin or anybody else. Blondie had admitted that much. But what could it be?

Try as I might, I couldn't figure out anything all that special about me. It couldn't be because I might tell somebody about them. Nobody would believe me anyway, and besides that, Justin had known about them for years and nobody had ever kidnapped him or caused him any problems just because he knew too much.

So if it wasn't that, then what was it? That part still baffled me.

I laid back on the mattress and laced my fingers together behind my head, staring up at the ceiling while I thought. It was one of those ceilings with blown plaster all over it with little sparkly things embedded, and they glittered in the light from the windows.

After a while that ceiling gave me an idea. Plaster is tough, but it's nowhere near as tough as concrete blocks. I might be able to knock a hole in it, if I could find something to do it with and a place where nobody could see me.

I knew the main room would never do, because of that danged window in the door. Anybody might walk by and see what I was doing, at any time. Even if I took my shirt off and used it to cover up the window, I figured that would be a surefire way to make the wolves suspicious enough to open the door and come in there, and if they did then it would wreck everything.

There was still the bathroom, though. I got up and moseyed in there and shut the rusty door behind me. That took care of not being seen. Sure enough, it had the same kind of ceiling as the other room, and I glanced around to see if there was anything I could use to dig a hole in it.

That bathroom was about as bare as a picked bone, I have to say. There was absolutely nothing in it except the commode, a sink, the bathtub, and a metal medicine cabinet which turned out to be completely empty. Nothing sharp or useful at all.

I thought about breaking the mirror on the medicine cabinet or smashing the lid of the toilet tank against the floor to get a sharp piece I could use, but I didn't waste half a second giving up on those ideas. Smashing things would make way too much noise, and I didn't dare attract attention. I thought longingly of my pocket knife, or one of the ten million screwdrivers Justin had in his workshop. I think I would even have settled for a paperclip at that point.

My pockets were stripped empty this time, though. The wolves had taken everything I had except for a few pieces of lint.

I wasn't ready to give up yet, though. I took the lid off the toilet tank and looked inside there. Toilets have a couple of moving parts, and sometimes a few of them are metal.

Just as I thought, there was a thin metal rod that connected the floater thingy to the water valve. I stuck my hand down inside the tank and found that I could unscrew the whole thing from the valve if I twisted hard enough. It was slimy and nasty and hard to keep hold of, but after a few minutes I had the metal rod loose, with the floater still attached to one end of it. The floater was supposed to unscrew from the rod the same way, but it had been on there so long it wouldn't come free.

I finally gave up trying to get it off. I had one sharp end, and that's all I needed.

I put the lid back where it came from and then gingerly climbed up on top of the tank itself. It was none too sturdy, and I had to be careful not to move too much because every time I did, the tank swayed and wobbled and acted like it was about to dump me on the floor. I used one hand to steady myself against the medicine cabinet till I was sure I wasn't going to fall.

When I was sure, I took the floater rod and started scratching at the ceiling right above me. It's hard to dig a hole in gypsum board, but if you're determined and if you've got something halfway sharp, you can do it.

Plaster dust kept sifting down on my face and making me want to sneeze, but at last the rod poked clean through to the other side. I went after it with doubled energy after that, till I made a hole big enough to stick my thumb through. I hooked a finger around the back of the plaster and pulled down. It wouldn't break and I was afraid to put my weight into it. I didn't want to go crashing to the floor if it broke loose all of a sudden.

I attacked it with the rod again, working all around the edges till I could get my three middle fingers inside. Then I pulled with all my strength, and just when I thought I was about to give myself a hernia, a palm-sized piece of plaster broke loose in my hand.

"Awesome," I said to myself, whispering so nobody could hear me.

I set the piece of plaster on top of the medicine cabinet and started breaking off more pieces. After that it didn't take long at all before I had a hole in the ceiling big enough for me to stick my head through, and finally it was big enough for my whole body.

I stopped my demolition work and reached up to grab hold of two rafters with my hands, and then I pulled myself up till I could sit on one of them. The whole thing only took maybe thirty minutes.

I found myself in a crawl space not much more than five feet high. It was awfully dark up there, and blistering hot, too. I could see rafters stretching off for a long way in both directions, and there was a metal roof right above me that was giving off heat like a demon. I was already sweating.

There was no use trying to hide the hole in the ceiling, so I didn't bother. If anybody came in the bathroom then my goose was cooked, plain and simple. And I knew sooner or later somebody *would* come, if only to check on me. That's why I didn't have a second to waste.

I stood up as best I could and started stepping carefully from rafter to rafter. That was ticklish business, because I knew if I stepped in the wrong place I'd end up crashing down through the plaster into the room below me.

That didn't happen though, because every so often there were ventilation grates that opened into the rooms below. They let in just enough light so I could sort of see where I was going, after my eyes adjusted.

They let noises come up into the attic, too, and when I heard Blondie's voice I froze for a second. She was talking to somebody in the room right under me, in that same prissy, superior tone I hated so much.

At first I was tempted to ignore her and go on my way, but then I heard my name.

"You might as well go ahead and tell me, honey. Zach already decided to help us," I heard her say. Maybe I'm too curious for my own good, but I couldn't help wondering what it was I was supposed to be helping them with. It was certainly news to *me*.

I forgot all about trying to get out of the attic, at least for the moment, and crept a little closer to the vent and leaned down close where I could hear better. It was a long shot, but there was always the chance I might learn something useful.

I could see into the room a little bit, but not enough to catch a glimpse of the girl or who she was talking to. All I could see was the edge of the sink in the bathroom and a slice of the open door.

"Laura, you're such a liar. If Zach already told you where it is then you wouldn't still be asking *me*. But you're wasting your time, because I already told you fifty million times I don't know anything," I heard someone else say. It was a boy's voice, and he sounded a little bit younger than me. That was all I could tell.

Right after that, I heard the sharp smack of a hand against bare skin. There was no way of mistaking what it was. There's nothing quite like that sound.

"You're so stupid, Cameron. You could save yourself so much pain and trouble if you'd just cooperate. You know we'll find it anyway sooner or later," she told him.

"I told you I don't know where it is," he said, in a voice that maybe shook a little bit but still sounded very sure. I could imagine the girl gritting her teeth, and then she slapped him again for good measure.

"That's a taste for later," she hissed. He didn't answer, and after a few seconds I heard her walking across the tile floor away from me.

"I'll leave you to think about that for a while. I'll be back later to see if you've changed your mind," she told him. I heard the door open and then slam shut behind her, and then the room below me was quiet.

I wondered why she'd been so nice to me earlier, if this was the way she treated her other prisoners. Maybe she was just waiting to see if I could be talked into doing what she wanted, and she'd only get nasty when she decided being nice wasn't going to work.

I don't like it when I see people getting mistreated. It makes me mad, and I want to do something about it if I can.

I made a quick decision.

"Hey kid. . . Cameron," I called out, torn between wanting him to hear me and not wanting my voice to carry too far. I don't think he heard me, so I called again, a little louder. That time I heard the bed creak.

"Who's there?" he said out loud.

"Don't say anything. Just come in the bathroom," I told him. He must have wondered what was up, but he didn't argue about it. After a few seconds I saw a boy in bare feet and a ratty white t-shirt come into the bathroom. There was a red hand print on his left cheek where Laura had slapped him twice. He had blond hair and he wasn't as young as I thought he was. He looked about the same age as me, more or less.

"Look up here. At the vent," I told him. He didn't act surprised. Just shut the bathroom door behind him and looked up at me. He had bright blue eyes almost exactly the same color as mine, and I remember thinking it was unusual at the time. I doubted he could see me in the dark attic, so I stuck my hand down close to the grate and waved at him. He'd be able to see motion at least.

"Who are you, and what are you doing up there?" he asked, getting right to the point.

"I'm here to help you get out of this place if you want to," I told him.

"Yeah? How?" he wanted to know.

"I'll break the ceiling plaster and you can climb up here in the attic with me. Just make sure it doesn't make any noise when it falls," I warned him.

It didn't take him long to make up his mind.

"Sure, I'm game," he said.

He quickly climbed up on the tank lid just like I had, and stood there ready to catch any pieces that might fall. I put one foot on the plaster right about where I judged his head was, and then gradually put more and more of my weight on it till I felt it start to crack. I was careful to keep my other foot on a rafter and hold on with both hands to the roof struts so I wouldn't fall through the ceiling when it broke.

Which it finally did. My foot punched through and I almost kicked Cameron in the face, if he hadn't ducked just in time. No big pieces fell, just a few little globs that didn't make enough noise to matter. Cameron grabbed the edges of the hole and pulled down several big chunks of plaster, and as soon as that was done, I gave him a hand and hauled him up into the attic with me.

"Come on, let's find a way out of here," I said. Introductions and chit-chat could wait till later. The wolves might discover one of us missing at any time. Cameron nodded without saying a word, and I went back to feeling my way through the dark.

It wasn't long before we came to the end of the building. There was a wooden louvered window there to let air circulate into the attic, but it also gave us a chance to see outside without anybody being able to tell we were there.

I peered through the cracks and saw a few other buildings and a couple of cars, but no people moving around. None of the buildings seemed to have windows except for those same little slits like I'd seen in my room. Maybe that's because it was a deer camp and they wanted to keep people from breaking in through the windows during off-season; I really don't know for sure. Whatever the reason was, it was a good thing for me and Cameron. Even if there were people inside those other buildings, they wouldn't be able to see us even after we got outside. We needed every piece of luck we could get.

But in the meantime, there was no way to get out through those dadgummed louvers. They were nailed together tight, and unless we had a hammer they were going to stay that way.

"Are we getting out this way?" Cameron whispered.

"I don't think we can, without a hammer or somethin'. Come on and let's look for the door instead. There's got to be one here somewhere," I whispered back.

I knew there had to be an access panel or a trap door or some such thing, if we could just find it. People had to come up there for maintenance and stuff now and then, didn't they?

We were both sweating so much by then it was running down and getting into our eyes and making them sting, and my whole t-shirt was soaked. I couldn't see Cameron well enough to tell whether he was as bad off as I was, but I'd be willing to bet on it. It was so hot it was hard to breathe, and I knew neither one of us could handle that for very long. We'd pass out from heat exhaustion if we didn't find a way out soon.

By and by we stumbled across an area where the floor was finished out with plywood, and there were some boxes and things stacked up. There was a trap door off to one side which I guess led down to the main floor of the building, but when Cameron tried to open it we soon found out it wouldn't move an inch. Locked, I'm sure.

"This thing's not coming open, dude. It won't even budge," he told me.

We felt around the edges of the door to see if there was a key or a latch or anything else that might let us open the trap and get out, but there wasn't anything. I bet it was probably locked with a hasp and a padlock down below, because when you got to thinking about it, why would anybody ever need to unlock the door from the top side?

At that point I was frustrated and starting to get a little scared that we wouldn't be able to find a way out, after all. I even seriously started to think about breaking down through the ceiling somewhere into one of the other rooms and trying to sneak out through the front door.

That's when I found the pipe.

It was just a stick of galvanized metal water pipe, old and rusty and no particular use to anybody, I don't guess. You know how attics always collect junk like that which nobody really gives a hoot about but nobody ever wants to throw away. The pipe was about three feet long, and the only reason I found it at all in the pitch dark was because I stepped on it and nearly brained myself on the rafters when it rolled out from under my foot.

Luckily I caught my balance before I killed myself, and when I groped around on the floor to see what it was I'd stepped on, I felt the pipe. I grabbed it in my hand and picked it up.

At first the only thing I had in mind was to use it for a weapon to defend myself if I had to. A piece of steel pipe can make a mighty fine club, in a pinch. It took me a few minutes before I realized it could make a mighty fine pry bar, too.

Chapter Four

"Come on, Cameron, I've got an idea," I told him.

We picked our way back to the louvered window and I stuck the metal pipe in between the slats, real close to one edge where the nails were. Then I pulled.

The nails made a horribly loud squealing noise when they pulled out of the wood, and I stopped, my heart pounding. It was so loud I was sure somebody down below would hear it and come find us.

"What's wrong? Why'd you stop?" Cameron asked.

"It's too loud. Somebody's bound to hear the noise," I whispered.

"Well pull slower then, but we have to get that window open, dude. There's no other way out and we got no time to look for one," he pointed out.

I know good sense when I hear it, so I bit my tongue and yanked hard on the bar. The nails came squealing out of the window frame, and before long I had one end of the board free. Cameron grabbed it and twisted it loose on the other side, and then he set it down carefully. The nails were making enough racket without dropping pieces of wood on the floor.

We yanked off six more louvers as fast as the walrus opened oysters, and then we had a space plenty big enough for us to fit through. I gave it one more wary look to make sure there was nobody around outside before I tore the screen loose. I didn't care about fixing it later; I just punched a hole in it with the metal pipe and then ripped it the rest of the way open the best I could.

It was maybe ten feet to the ground, but that couldn't be helped. I put my feet through first and then my body, till I was standing on the outside of the windowsill.

It looked a lot farther down than it really was. Maybe that's just because I don't like heights very much, but this time I didn't have any choice. I took a deep breath and jumped.

With my eyes shut.

It kinda hurt when I landed, but I was ready for that. I dropped and rolled to take some of the force off my feet, so that helped. As long as I didn't twist an ankle I was good to go.

The first thing I did when I got outside was to slick myself right up against the wall of the building and look around to see if anybody had noticed me jumping out of the window.

I didn't see or hear anything unusual, so I relaxed just a tiny bit. To tell the truth, it felt so good to be out in the cool air after nearly roasting to death in that attic, it was hard to think of anything else. I took deep breaths and just gloried in it for a whole ten seconds before I remembered we weren't out of the woods just yet.

I waved to Cameron to come on down, which he did. He didn't land quite as well as I did and ended up tearing a hole in the knee of his jeans and skinning his left palm. I knew it had to hurt, but he joined me against the wall without saying anything about it.

"You okay, bud?" I asked.

"Yeah, I'm good. Just stings a little, that's all," he said. He took his shirt tail and pressed it against his palm so it would quit bleeding.

The dark blue Blazer was parked maybe twenty feet away at the corner of the building we were next to, and that gave me an idea.

We slid along the wall as smooth as a melted Mars bar, till we got up close beside the car. Then I stealthily reached up and grabbed the door handle, and when I tried it I found that it was unlocked.

I motioned for Cameron to get in, and then I slipped into the driver's seat behind him and shut the door without slamming it. Those dark-tinted windows helped a lot now, since it meant nobody could see us inside unless they came really close.

There was an insurance card clipped on the dashboard that said the Blazer belonged to somebody named Janelle Parker from West Memphis. I'd never heard of her, but you never could tell when it might turn out to be a useful little tidbit of information.

It was more than I'd dared to hope for, but this time the keys were sitting in the cup holder on the console. Whoever drove the Blazer last time wasn't as careful as he should have been. Maybe he didn't think there was any reason to be careful about leaving the keys lying around, not this far back in the woods and with me and Cameron locked up tight.

Good enough. I picked them up, a little nervous. Every vehicle handles a little bit different, and I'd never tried to drive anything this big and bulky before. So yeah, honestly I was more than a little nervous. Cameron looked at me skeptically.

"Are you sure you're okay to drive?" he finally asked.

"Sure, I can drive just fine," I promised. He didn't look like he was totally convinced, but he didn't say anything else about it. We were both barefooted, and I'm sure he didn't want to try to run off through the woods like that. I know I didn't. I remembered what it felt like the last time.

I stuck the key in the ignition and started the engine. It was a quiet one, thankfully, so I was pretty sure nobody could hear it. I pulled the door shut real slow till I felt the lock click, and then I put the Blazer in reverse and backed up till I had enough room to clear the corner of the building. The brakes were touchier than I was used to and I skidded on gravel when I tried to stop too fast. Stupid greenhorn trick, that was, and I glanced at Cameron to see if he noticed.

He didn't seem to be paying any attention, so I put the Blazer in drive and headed out of there. I didn't drive too fast and I was careful not to do anything else to attract attention. The whole place looked emptier than a bum's billfold, but I still had that creepy feeling of being watched. You know how you can always tell when somebody's eyes are on you. It felt like that.

Maybe I was imagining things.

But then again, maybe not. We got to the gate where the camp ended and the dirt road began, and Cameron had to get out and open it. It was one of those big aluminum cattle gates and it wasn't locked, just held shut with a twist of yellow nylon rope to keep it from blowing open in the wind.

But anyway, *somebody* must have been watching us, because while Cameron was fumbling with the gate I heard a shout somewhere behind us. The game was up!

Cameron heard it too, and he didn't waste any more time trying to be quiet. He hauled off and kicked the gate open the rest of the way, then ran for the passenger side door.

He jumped in, and I spun gravel and sideswiped the gate on the way out. It hadn't finished opening all the way and I didn't have time to keep from hitting it. I heard metal screeching, and it left two or three long ugly scratches along the side of the Blazer.

"Go! Go!" Cameron yelled.

"I'm going!" I yelled right back.

To tell you the truth, I was terrified. Driving Justin's truck on back roads was slow and easy and he was always there to help me if I needed it. This was nothing like that. In fact, this was a nightmare. The pine trees were crowded close on both sides of the road, and there were deep ditches I was pretty sure I couldn't get out of if I slid into one. So I gripped the steering wheel tight in both hands and kept my eyes glued to the road, trying to keep from killing both of us.

Cameron didn't seem like he was worried about my driving, though. He had his window down and was looking behind us.

"Uh-oh. Here they come," he said. That was the last thing I wanted to hear, but there was nothing I could do about it right then except keep driving. I thought I was getting the hang of the Blazer by then, but learning how to drive while you're flying down a dirt road in the mountains with a pack of wolves hot on your tailpipe is not the easiest thing in the world to do. Try it yourself sometime if you don't believe me.

I had no idea where I was going, but the road snaked on through the woods with no turns or forks in sight, so I didn't have much chance to get lost. There were sometimes side roads that branched off, but they were all weedy and overgrown and I knew better than to turn off onto any of them. That wouldn't do anything but get us caught when we hit a dead end or a fallen log or a wash-out or anything else that blocked the way. If a road looks like nobody ever uses it, then that probably means it doesn't lead anywhere. I was also afraid of getting lost and driving in circles. The smartest thing to do was to keep on straight ahead.

I hoped.

The roads were dry as dust, and the Blazer kicked up so much dirt behind us that I guess it was choking the wolves to death. They dropped back a pretty good distance, so much that we even lost sight of them for a few minutes now and then around curves and over hills. That was good, sort of, even though I knew we'd never lose them that way. The dust cloud would always show them which way we went.

After a while we crested a little ridge and came to a T in the road that looked an awful lot like the one I saw yesterday when I was on foot. In fact I was ninety-nine percent sure it was the same one. If it was, then I needed to turn left to get to the highway.

I didn't have much time to think about it, but for some reason I turned right this time instead. I'm not sure why. The wolves were out of sight behind us, so maybe I was hoping they'd take the wrong fork when they came to that place. They had to know where the highway was, and they had to be pretty sure I knew. They'd probably guess that's where I was headed. The new road also had more gravel and less dirt than the one we just came from, so we wouldn't kick up near as much of a dust cloud as we had been. It was a slim hope, but it was better than none at all.

I turned too fast and the Blazer fishtailed on the gravel and I almost lost control and hit the ditch. I had to slam on the brakes and almost stop before I dared go on.

Cameron's eyes were big as dinner plates and my hands were shaking from the close call, but there was nothing we could do except to keep going.

I drove slower for a while, partly so we'd kick up less dust and partly to settle my nerves after that almost-wreck. The wolves never did catch up with us again after that, and I almost dared to hope we'd lost them by turning this way.

After what seemed like a long time we started passing houses once in a while. Then all of a sudden the road turned to pavement, and that was even better. No more dust trail or tire tracks to give us away to anybody who might be following us, and we could go faster, too.

Several miles later we came to a bridge, and just upstream I recognized the little beach where the people in the pickup truck had been parked yesterday afternoon when I floated by in that leaky tube. It seemed like a month ago.

I knew where I was, then. This was the Caddo River again, and all I needed to do was head south on the highway that ran beside it. So that's what I did, and within another ten minutes we were back in Glenwood.

At first it was hard for me to believe it had been that easy, but I wasn't dumb enough to think it was over yet. I was sure the wolves wouldn't give up that soon. They had to have another trick or two up their nasty little sleeves, and that's what worried me. Not knowing what might happen is always the hardest part of any bad situation, you know.

But the Blazer was running low on gas, and I didn't really have a driver's license anyway, and all we had was three bucks in change that Cameron found in the ashtray. That wouldn't be anywhere near enough to get back home, that's for sure. Not to mention the fact that we were driving a stolen car, sort of. I hoped it might get us another ten or twenty miles down the road so we'd be harder to find, but after that I didn't know what we'd do.

"We've got to ditch this car, dude," Cameron said.

"What, you mean like right now? How come? I think we lost them back there on the dirt road, at least for a while," I told him. He was already shaking his head before I even finished.

"Not for long we didn't. This is my mom's car. It's got OnStar and she'll find out exactly where we are as soon as she gets a chance to call them. She doesn't have cell service up in the mountains but she will as soon as she gets closer to town," he said.

I sighed. I knew it had been too easy. No wonder they hadn't followed us harder.

Cameron popped open the glove box and rooted around a few seconds until he pulled out a red mp3 player and a set of ear buds, then slipped them in his pocket.

"Might as well take this, you know. It's mine anyway," he said.

Just then the engine died. I guess Cameron's mom must have reached a place where her cell phone worked, and she called OnStar and had them kill the motor. It also meant she knew exactly where we were, and the wolves would be right on top of us in a matter of minutes.

The Blazer was still rolling, so I turned the wheel and managed to pull into a parking slot in front of the Diamond Bank. It was closed and we were the only car in the parking lot. Nobody could possibly overlook us if they drove by on the highway. I wished we could have found a place where we didn't stick out like a bug on a plate, but oh well. I tested the engine again just to make sure, and it was deader than road kill.

We were in a pretty tight spot, but in spite of everything I actually felt pretty cocky for pulling off my third great escape in two days. I remembered Laura calling me a slippery little fish back at the deer camp, and I wished I could have been there to see the look on her face when she found my room empty. I smiled a little, just imagining it. They didn't know who they were dealing with!

Yeah, I was really thinking stuff like that at the time, much as it embarrasses me to admit it now. I hope I'm not that full of myself all the time.

But busting out was one thing, and staying that way was a whole 'nother matter. So far I hadn't done too well at that half of the problem. That was enough to knock me back down to reality, when I thought about it.

We jumped out of the car, but instead of hightailing it away from there, Cameron yanked open the back door and started digging through the trash in the back seat.

"What are you doing, boy? We've got to get away from here!" I said.

"We've got to find the journal and the maps first. I know they're in here somewhere. I almost forgot about it, but we can't leave without them," he said.

He might as well have been speaking Greek for all I knew, but there was no time to ask questions or fight about it.

Sometimes you have to just trust people, you know. It's not always easy and you can't always have a reason for it. Cameron knew the danger as well as I did, so if there was something in the back seat so important that he was willing to risk getting caught just to find it, then I had to believe it was worth it, too. I opened the door on my side and started digging.

The Blazer was full of junk, and most of it was just trash. Nobody saves McDonald's bags for any good reason that I can think of. I wasn't sure exactly what I was supposed to be looking for, but I was pretty sure it wasn't burger wrappers.

I couldn't pay attention like I should have, because I kept wanting to look at the highway to see if anybody was slowing down. Nobody did, but I was antsy anyway. We probably had at least five minutes or so before the wolves could possibly get there, but you never knew for sure. I wanted to get gone.

I don't like piggy people who fill up their cars like trash cans. It makes it stink inside and it's just nasty. The Blazer was like that, and more than once I wanted to hold my nose while I dug through there. Somebody had left half a cheeseburger on the seat, and it had been there so long it was dried out like a piece of wood. I almost hurled when I came across that little jewel.

It seemed like it took forever, but really it couldn't have been more than a minute or so before I found a US Geological Survey section map for southern Montgomery County with several spots marked on it in red ink and others in pencil. It looked like the red ones had been pencil to start with, and then marked over with a red pen later on. I couldn't make hide nor hair of what it was supposed to mean or why those particular spots were marked. They all looked like they were out in the middle of nowhere to me.

There were two other section maps rolled up with the first one, and they were marked with those same pencil scribbles in various places, but no red marks. I didn't take the time to look any closer.

I know how to read section maps because Justin uses them a lot when he has to go out and do field work. Oil wells don't always have nice neat addresses on streets, and sometimes you have to use topographical maps to find them instead. He used to take me with him now and then and he taught me how to read his maps so I could give him directions. I never really thought much about it before, but now I was glad I learned.

"Hey Cameron, is this what you're looking for?" I asked him, holding up the first section map.

"Yeah, that's it! We have to find the journal too, though," he said.

I folded up the maps and stuck them in my front pocket. They made a big bulky wad of paper, but it was still better than carrying them.

Right under the maps there was a school notebook with some writing in it that I didn't have time to read, but I grabbed that too without even asking Cameron if it was important.

Then I found what had to be the journal. It was a very old-looking book with crumbly pages which was shoved down there next to the rotten cheeseburger in the middle of the seat. It was bound in cracked brown leather, and it was partly burnt on one of the bottom corners. Cameron saw it at the same time I did and snatched it up.

Then he brushed aside some trash on the floorboard and grabbed a skateboard out from underneath it.

"Have you got anything *else* in there you want to take?" I asked, with just a touch of irritation.

"Nah, that's all, dude. It's just this was expensive and I didn't want to leave it. But let's get out of here," he said, slamming the back door.

I made sure to lock the doors before we left, and then I threw the keys into some thick azalea bushes in front of the bank. A storm drain would have been even better, but I didn't see one handy. The more time they wasted dealing with the Blazer, the better.

"Come *on,* dude. We don't have time for all that," Cameron said, looking out at the highway behind us. It couldn't have been more than five minutes since we parked the Blazer, but he was acting scared and I can't say I blamed him.

"All right, let's go," I agreed.

We took off at a fast run, getting behind the bank first and then crossing through some trees until we came to another street. I still didn't feel safe, so we kept going for quite a while, even ducking through back yards and alleys when we had to, to help stay out of sight. We got barked at by several dogs, but that was about it.

"Dang, this thing gets heavy after a while," Cameron said, setting his skateboard down on the pavement. We were walking down a narrow alley between two buildings where nobody was likely to see us, and it seemed like a good place to stop and rest. He was a little out of breath from running, but then so was I.

"Yeah, let's take a break for a few minutes. I think we're safe here," I said. He sat down on his board, and I found an old plastic milk crate to sit on. The alley was full of crud like that, so it wasn't hard to find something.

"So what now?" Cameron asked after a while.

"We need to find a phone so I can call my uncle. He'll come get us and then we can figure out what to do once we're safe away from here," I told him.

"You're sure he'd come?" Cameron asked.

"Yeah, I live with him. He wouldn't let me down," I said confidently.

"You must be Zach, then," he said. That's when I suddenly remembered I'd never actually told him who I was. There hadn't been time.

"Uh, yeah. That's me. How'd you know?" I asked.

"Aw, I've been around awhile. I hear things. I'm Cameron Parker, by the way," he said, sticking his hand out. I shook it because it would have been rude not to, but I couldn't help wondering about him anyway, now that I had time to think about it. His mother was the one who owned the Blazer, which meant she was either a *loup-garou* herself or else she was in cahoots with them some kind of way. So what did that mean about Cameron, then?

I think I would have had a hard time trusting him, except for one thing. I knew he'd been locked up at the deer camp, the same way I was. I'd seen the way Laura slapped him and I'd heard the way she talked to him. After all that, it was hard for me to believe he was just a mole-rat. And like I said, sometimes you just have to trust people, even when it's hard.

Still, I couldn't help glancing at his fingernails just to make sure. He noticed, and held them up so I could see better. They were normal, just like mine.

"Nope, they never changed me yet," he said, half smiling. I was embarrassed that he caught me looking, but at least he seemed to think it was funny instead of getting mad at me.

"You seem like you know a lot of things," I finally said, lamely. I wasn't sure what else to say. Cameron just shrugged.

"I know what I know, that's all," he said. It was a cryptic thing to say, and I didn't feel like leaving it at that. In spite of what I said about trusting him, I had to know more.

"Then tell me what this is all about, if you can," I asked.

"That would be a long story, dude," he said.

"I've got nothing better to do than listen," I pointed out.

"Well. . . true 'nuff. I'm your third cousin, to start with. That's why I know some of the things I know. My grandpa and yours were brothers," he said matter-of-factly.

There didn't seem to be a lot I could say about that right then, but you can bet I tucked it away in the back of my mind to think about later.

"All right. I guess that explains how you got hooked up with the wolves and why you know some stuff about me. But why'd they have you locked up, and what do they want with *me*?" I asked. Those were the things I really wanted to hear about.

"Oh, I know what they want *you* for. They think you know where the Sweet Spring is," he said. That didn't do anything but confuse me even more.

"Laura said it was because they wanted me to become a *loup-garou* after all," I said.

"Well. . . maybe that too, but that's not the main reason. She was probably just telling you something she thought you'd believe until she decided how much to trust you. Laura's really good at messing with your head, you know. You can't trust anything she says," he said.

None of that surprised me. I already knew better than to believe anything Laura said. But I didn't care about that; I wanted to hear more about the Sweet Spring, whatever *that* was.

"Okay, so what's the Sweet Spring?" I asked, getting right to the point.

Cameron looked at me curiously for a few seconds.

"You really don't know, do you?" he finally said, shaking his head.

"Nope, I'm afraid not," I told him.

"Hmm. . . Well, I guess it *would* be hard to swallow all at once, if you didn't know anything," he said, half to himself, "But never mind. They've been trying to find that spring for years and years. I don't know exactly what it does, but it's important because there's a prophecy or something about it. They say one of the boys in the seventh generation is supposed to use it to break the curse. That's either me or you, and- " he said.

"Whoa, slow down a minute. Seventh generation of *what*? And *who* says all that?" I asked. I felt like the ground had opened up at my feet and left me standing on the edge of a deep ocean of weirdness.

"You don't even know about *that?*" he asked, like he couldn't believe it. It made me feel stupid, and I hate feeling that way.

"No, I guess I don't. Tell me," I said, trying to be polite. Cameron shrugged again in that way he does.

"All right, Zach. There's not really that much more to tell anyway. A long time ago, a man named Daniel Trewick figured out how to become the first *loup-garou*, or at least the first one in our family. I'm not real sure about that part. But *he* always said one of his great-great-great-great grandsons would either break the curse or renew it, whatever that means. That's seven generations. He also said the Curse-Breaker would have a mark on him so they'd know which boy it was," he said.

"What was the mark?" I whispered.

"Bright blue eyes, just like yours and mine," he said, with a laugh that didn't sound like he thought it was very funny.

"But that's stupid. Anybody could have blue eyes," I objected.

"*You* try telling them that. They won't listen, I promise you," he said.

"Anyway, there are only two of us who fit the bill, just me and you," he went on.

"How do you know all this?" I asked him for the second time. I'd never heard anything remotely like it in my life. I used to think my parents never told me anything when I was younger, but I never imagined how *much* they didn't tell me.

"Well, if you hadn't run away then you'd know at least that much yourself. That's something everybody in the family has to learn. You can read more about it in the journal sometime if you really want to," he said.

"Okay then, go on," I said.

"Anyway, they never could make up their minds which one of us it was. Everybody was already real suspicious of you and why you didn't want to be like everybody else, and then when you ran away that clinched it. They were all sure you must be the Curse-

Breaker. It took the heat off me a little bit, and for a while they forgot about everything else except trying to find you and stop you from wrecking things. That's why they wouldn't give up till they had you. You did an awful good job of hiding, I have to say. We like to have never found you," he said.

"You helped them?" I accused.

"Well, yeah, I kinda had to, you know. They would have started looking at *me* funny again if I hadn't. Just because they were sure you were the one didn't mean they forgot I was a suspect, too," he pointed out.

"Well, yeah, I can see that. So what happened next?" I asked.

"Oh, I got careless, said some things I shouldn't have, did some things I was stupid to have done. Made them wonder. And then they finally did catch you and found out you didn't seem to have a clue what was up, so then they started getting all narrow-eyed and suspicious about *me* again. They couldn't decide which one of us it was, so they locked us both up just to make sure. They don't take chances about stuff like that, Zach," he said quietly.

I chewed on all that for a while. Cameron didn't seem like he wanted to add anything else to what he'd already said, but there was one more thing I had to know.

"So why'd you help me then?" I finally asked, just as quietly.

"Well, why'd you help *me*, when you didn't know who I was or why I was there? You took a chance on getting caught and maybe worse, just for me. I've had to live my whole life being looked at like I was a stray dog that might turn and bite somebody any minute, 'cause they all wondered if I was the Curse-Breaker. Even my mom looks at me that way. She thinks I don't see it, but I do. I'm tired of it, Zach. I just want to be normal for a while, if I can be, and you're the first person I can remember who ever treated me that way," he said.

I didn't know what to say to that. I knew exactly what he was talking about and how he felt. He felt rejected. He knew more about the reasons behind it than I ever did, but I guess that doesn't make it hurt any less. There's no reason good enough to excuse it, and nothing anybody can say to fill up that empty spot. I knew it all too well.

But I thought I understood him now.

So I didn't say anything, just clapped him on the right shoulder and left it at that. Sometimes you say the most when you say the least.

Chapter Five

That's how me and Cameron got to be friends. It had been a really long time since I had one. I think I was afraid to get too close to anybody in Texarkana, because I never felt really safe doing that. Not with Justin and Eileen, but with other kids I mean. Friendship is a kind of love, you know, and love is always risky business. I think when I lost so much of what I had and so many people I cared about, I just wanted to keep from getting hurt like that again.

I'm not sure why Cameron was any different. Maybe it's because he went through so many of the same things I did, or maybe it's because he was family, or maybe it was something else completely. I don't really know. Sometimes two people join together like drops of water on a windowpane, and you don't even notice when you became friends. It just seems like you always have been. I hadn't felt that way about anybody since I left Jonathan in Tennessee.

I didn't say any of that out loud, of course. It was hard enough to think it all through myself, and it feels weird to talk about stuff like that with another boy. You know what you're trying to say, and maybe he does too, but it's just awkward for some reason. Maybe it shouldn't be, but that's the way it is.

"Well, I'm glad you came along," I said after a little while. It sounded dumb even to me, but it was the best thing I could come up with at the time. Cameron sorta laughed.

"Yeah, me too, Zach," he said.

We had to walk a long time before we found a phone. Probably because we were still afraid to go anywhere near the main roads, and you don't often find payphones on back streets. Now and then we didn't have any choice but to get out in plain view and that always made us jumpy, but nothing happened.

I wished I still had my cell phone. I guess the wolves took it when they locked me up. That worried me a little bit because I sure didn't want them getting the numbers off my contact list or having any more information about me than they already did. They already knew way too much. I hoped it never started working again after it got dunked in the river.

Anyway, after maybe an hour or so we came to an Exxon station with a payphone out front. It was at a busy intersection with cars and people everywhere, just exactly the kind of place we'd been trying to stay away from. There was nowhere to hide and no place to run to, if anybody saw us.

"This is not good," I said.

"Do you have a better idea?" Cameron pointed out reasonably. I knew he was right, but I still didn't like it.

"Well. . . you stay here behind the fence just in case the wolves nab me. That way you might could do something to help me if you had to. If they catch both of us then we're out of luck," I finally said.

I didn't give him time to say anything else. I quickly slipped around the edge of the wooden fence and across the parking lot, trying to look as natural and carefree as I could. I made it to the phone without anything happening, and I punched in Justin's number. I had to use some of the change we took from the Blazer or I wouldn't have been able to call him at all.

This time he picked up on the first ring.

I think he knew it was me before he even answered the phone. I'm not sure *how* he knew, unless maybe he guessed it from the number on his caller ID, but however he knew, he knew.

"Are you okay?" was the first thing he said.

"Yeah, I'm fine. But come get me as quick as you can, though. The wolves are after me and they could be anywhere," I told him.

"Where are you?" he asked me.

One thing I have to say about Justin. He never asks for long explanations when it's not the right time for it. He just does whatever needs to be done and then waits to talk about the details later.

"I'm at the Exxon station in Glenwood at the corner of Broadway and Highway 8. You can't miss it," I said.

"I'll be there in five minutes," he said. That sorta shocked me; I hadn't known he was already in town. But then again maybe I shouldn't have been surprised. I already left him that message on his voicemail yesterday from the gas station in Norman, and then again from the phone at the grocery store last night. He must have left Houston to come look for me as soon as he got the messages, and then I guess he drove all night to get here, wondering where I was and what happened to me after that last call.

Sometimes people do things like that and it catches you off guard how much they love you. I wish it wasn't so hard to remember it all the time.

I waved to Cameron to come out from behind the fence, and we went inside the store to wait. It was safer in there than it was in the parking lot, if anybody saw us. There was a Subway Sandwich place in the corner, and we sat down at one of the booths. We were screened off from the street by a rack of candy bars and potato chips, so it was about as good a hiding place as we could hope for.

Justin was as good as his word, and it probably wasn't even five minutes before he came walking through the door. He must have been really close already.

He saw me sitting at the booth by the Subway place, and before I could even finish standing up he had me wrapped in a rib-crushing bear hug.

Everybody in the store turned to look at us, and all those warm fuzzy feelings I'd been having a few minutes ago wore off pretty quick.

"I'm good, dude. Put me down," I said, probably a little gruffer than I really meant to. He did, and then he looked at Cameron and raised his eyebrow.

"This is Cameron. He's running from the wolves too. I'll tell you everything later, but right now we need to get out of here as quick as we can," I told him.

Like I said before, Justin is really good about sticking to what matters. Safety was the main thing right then, so everything else could wait.

"All right, Zach. Come on, boys. Let's get out of here while we still can," he said.

We got outside and I saw that he'd parked crooked and left the truck door wide open, he was in such a hurry to get inside the store a little bit faster. Cameron climbed in the back seat and I took the passenger side, and for the first time in days I felt safe again.

It wasn't till we were completely out of town on the highway headed home that Justin asked me what was going on.

I told him everything that happened since the night they grabbed me in the back yard, and he was just as confused as I was about most of it. Cameron told him about the Sweet Spring and the prophecy and everything, but that only made it seem stranger and more complicated than it already was.

"Maybe now's the time to look at those books and papers you got out of the Blazer. They might tell us somethin'," Justin finally suggested.

It sounded like a good idea, so I pulled the wad of papers out of my pants pocket and smoothed them out. The maps wouldn't take as long to look at as the notebook or the journal, so they seemed like the best place to start.

They didn't seem like anything special, when I looked; just old topographical survey maps with a bunch of pencil marks on them in strange places.

"The pencil marks are the places where Mom and Laura thought the spring might be, and the red ones are the places they already checked," Cameron said.

"Why just those places and no others?" I asked.

"All I know is that all of them are close to a place named Wolf Mountain. They never would tell me very much about it," he said.

I set the maps aside before long and opened the notebook, which turned out to be field notes they made about what they found at all those places on the maps. Dry, boring stuff that didn't really help too much.

"Here, Zach. Read the journal for us," Cameron told me. He'd been carrying it ever since he took it out of the Blazer, and now he handed it to me between the seats.

I took it from him carefully, like it might fall apart if I handled it too rough. Then I opened it to page one, and what I found in there changed my life.

It wasn't what I expected. I can say that much. It wasn't even a printed book, come to find out. It was one of those blank diary-type books that you write in, which is what somebody had done with this one.

The writing was really old. I think I would have known that even if the book wasn't yellow and cracked with age, because the letters looked funny. If you've ever seen an old person's handwriting, you know they don't usually write the same way we do nowadays. Their letters are all flowery and full of curly-cues and long tails and things we don't use much anymore. It makes it hard to read sometimes.

I knew all that because when me and Justin tore out the old wallpaper in the back bedroom last summer we found some writing on the wallboards behind it from somebody who lived in the house a long time ago, and I remember it looked like that. I guess it stuck in my mind because at the time I thought it was sorta cool.

Anyway, the person who wrote the journal made his letters that way. I had trouble reading it, and I felt like I was in kindergarten all over again and just learning how to put words together. Even aside from that, it was faded and smudgy and not easy to read in other ways.

There was a name on the front page, but all I could make out was the first part, Daniel. The last name started with Tr- but the rest was too smudged to tell what it was. From what Cameron told me I guessed it was probably Daniel Trewick, my however-many great grandfather. I couldn't read the date on the first page, but on the second page the entry said March 3, 1842. I whistled under my breath. That was a long time ago.

It started out duller than dirt, to tell the truth. I found out a lot about Daniel and the stuff he did every day and what he thought about things, but not much that I really wanted to know. He was 14 years old when he started the journal and he lived on a cotton plantation just outside Shreveport, Louisiana.

History is not really one of those things that interests me a whole lot. I don't hate it or anything, but it's not something that grabs ahold of me, either. The more I read, the less I understood why the journal would be so interesting to anybody. I didn't remotely care that Beck the horse had a lame foot in June of 1842 after he stepped on a loose rock or that the Red River flooded that winter. I couldn't figure out why the wolves cared about such things either, unless all of them were secret history buffs.

But I knew they *did* care, so I didn't quit. I had to skim a lot of it, partly because it was so utterly boring and partly because it was almost impossible to read in a lot of places.

"Are you sure this is the right book?" I asked Cameron after a while.

"Yeah, I'm sure. Just keep reading," he said.

I was maybe halfway through the book when I found what I was looking for. It was May of 1845 by then, and Daniel was 16 years old and already in college in New Orleans. They started young back then, I guess.

By then he wasn't writing about lame horses and flooded cotton fields anymore. He was talking about magic and demons and stuff like that, and when I saw the word *loup-garou* my ears pricked up and I paid close attention.

Before long, I knew more about werewolves than I really wanted to. The journal listed all the plants you needed to use to make the chest paint for the cursing ceremony, and it described exactly how to do it and what day it had to be, and it said the blood had to be fresh, and that the cursed person had to kill something warm-blooded to finish the process. That kind of stuff brought back a lot of bad memories, but I bit my tongue and kept reading.

The journal went on to talk about where the ceremony had to take place for it to work, and for the first time I learned that not just anywhere would do. There were just a few certain places. It listed all the ones Daniel knew about, with maps to find them.

The first one was in Greggton, Texas, a town I had never heard of. I reminded myself to look it up later when I had a chance. Another one was in Caddo Gap, Arkansas. That one wasn't far from the deer camp where the wolves had kept me and Cameron locked up, and when I looked at the map a little closer I was pretty sure it *was* the deer camp, or very close to it. The third one was in Ruston, Louisiana. The fourth one was in Lebanon, Tennessee. That one made my blood run cold; that's where Mama and Daddy lived, and the map for that one looked an awful lot like the apple orchard behind their house. I always used to wonder why they picked Tennessee when they moved away from Texas. I guess they didn't want to get too far away from one of the cursing spots, and they must have known that one was there.

The last one was in Poplar Bluff, Missouri. The journal didn't explain why it was just those five particular places and no others. There was one more at a place called the New Camp, but there was a piece of the page missing after that, so I couldn't tell where that one was. I wasn't sure whether somebody had ripped it out on purpose or if that old paper had just flaked apart at some point.

Not all those towns even existed in 1845, but it looked like somebody with different handwriting had marked them on the maps later on. Somebody had put a question mark next to the part about the New Camp, so that made me think the wolves didn't know where that one was either. Maybe they didn't really care that much, since they had the other five.

It would be dull to tell you everything I read in the journal. I'm not even sure I *want* everybody to know. I'd rather not remember it myself. It's enough to say that Daniel found his way to that place in Greggton late one October, and then he took the curse that made him a *loup-garou* forever after. I think that was the scariest part of that whole book, that somebody would willingly choose to do such a thing, and spend so much time and effort to figure out how to go about it.

He did, though, and before long he gathered up a handful of other people who joined him. He was rich, and I guess money can buy you a lot of friends. Some things never change, do they?

The journal went on to talk about some of the hunts they had and how they cruised up the Red River by boat as far as Fulton and downstream as far as Rapides Parish every month on the nights when there was a full moon. Probably so nobody around Shreveport would notice anything, no doubt. I guess they had a rip-roaring good time there for a while. It sure sounded like it, from the way the journal was written.

Daniel's last entry was on October 2, 1863, when he was 35 years old, and all it said was that the whole group was supposed to be staying at the New Camp (wherever that was) for a few days later that month because somebody had to have their Ceremony done. That was all he wrote.

There was no way of knowing what happened to Daniel after that, but I guess there were lots of things that could make you bite the dust pretty suddenly back then. It wasn't a very safe time to be alive.

The book itself didn't end, though. There were at least twenty pages after that, mostly written by Daniel's son John. He became a *loup-garou* too, but everything seemed to fall to pieces without Daniel there to lead them. There were no more big hunts, no more talk about cruises on the Red River, nothing like that. John lost everything when the Civil War ended, and the wolves scattered out from Shreveport and had to fend for themselves as best they could. John ended up farming in Longview, Texas, which I found out later isn't far from Greggton.

It made me think. I knew Daddy was from Sulphur Springs, which was maybe an hour's drive or less from Longview. I guess the family must have hung around that area all those years. The book didn't say so, but I thought it was a pretty good hunch.

Most of the rest of the journal was family trees and names and addresses of werewolves, sometimes crossed out or updated or with little notes in the margins like when they died or something, penciled in by several different people with different handwriting. It was a lot less interesting after that, but I did notice one thing. Most of the people in the lists didn't seem to live all that long. Maybe it's dangerous, being a werewolf. Too many people out there with silver bullets and such, I guess.

I'm not sure why it surprised me when I found the name Maralyn Johnson on the third-from-last page, but there she was, with an address on Stonewall Street in Sulphur Springs, Texas, which somebody had crossed out later and filled in with Lebanon, Tennessee. It was Nana Maralyn. I slid my finger down a little bit to the name under hers- Anthony Trewick, and next to him, Jenna Wilder. My mom and dad. And under them, me and Lola. Somebody had circled my name with a red pen.

I stopped reading and stared at the book for a long time. Sometimes you just don't know what to think or say, you know? I sure didn't.

I noticed there were only ten living *loup-garous* still listed in the book, not counting the kids who were too young to be one yet. My mom and dad and Nana Maralyn, her nieces Lena and Janelle, their husbands, and Lena's three daughters, Laura, Michelle, and Lisa. Lisa had a husband named Logan Tygart, but he wasn't a *loup-garou* yet. There was a date under his name for sometime next month, and I guessed he was having to wait for the Hunter's Moon before he could be cursed.

After I saw that, I had a dirty hunch I knew who it was who grabbed me in the back yard. No wonder the silver didn't work on him.

"Was it Logan Tygart who snatched me?" I asked out loud. I guess it didn't really matter much, at that point, but I wanted to know. I still had a special grudge against Mr. Hairy Paws.

"Yeah, I'm sure it was. He's big and strong and he knows how to knock people out real quick, cause he's a vet. Why do you ask?" Cameron said. I have to admit, that's one job I never would have expected a werewolf to have. I thought a vet was supposed to love animals, not hunt them down and eat them alive. It just didn't seem to fit very well, you know. But on the other hand, it did explain a lot.

"So what's that stuff he knocked me out with? Cat tranquilizer?" I asked, thinking about the dart and the needle.

"Yeah, something like that. Probably horse tranquilizer, though. Logan only works with big animals, not little ones," he explained.

I let it go at that, but I promised myself I'd have some choice words for Doctor Logan Hairy-Paws Tygart when I got the chance.

Cameron was listed under Janelle, and I noticed his name was circled in red, too. There were other names, but they were little kids. I didn't recognize any of them, although I'm sure everybody had to stay in touch at least now and then.

I don't remember us ever having company at home when I was little, except for once. I'd almost forgotten about it until I saw the name Laura Beckham and the word Alabama. It's funny how little things like that will remind you of stuff you almost forgot.

But anyway, I can just barely remember a tall lady and her daughter coming to stay with us for two or three days on a night when the moon was full. I guess she was there to use the flat rock in the orchard when she became a *loup-garou,* and now I realized why the Laura at the deer camp looked so familiar for some reason. She was a lot older now, but she was the same girl who came to our house seven or eight years ago to have her curse done. Our rock in Lebanon was the closest one to their place in Huntsville.

When I was younger, I can remember wishing I knew more about my family, but I think now what I really wanted was to find out they were good people that I could look up to and admire for something. I wanted them to be kind and brave and to love God. Finding out they were all wrapped up in something I hated was hard to swallow.

I thought that's all there was to the book, but on the last page there was one more scribble. It looked like Daniel's writing again, and all it said was *"The water from the sweet spring breaks the curse."* There was a hasty map penciled in underneath it, but it was so smudged and old that I couldn't make head nor tails of it. The only feature I could read was labeled "Wolf Mountain", and there had to be at least a thousand of those around.

Out of curiosity, I picked up one of the section maps again and looked it over. Sure enough, there was a Wolf Mountain on it, not far from where all the spots were marked. I unrolled the other two and found out they both had places named Wolf Mountain too.

I thought about all that for a while.

So the wolves were looking for this "sweet spring", because the water could break the curse. Now I knew perfectly well that Mama and Daddy and Nana Maralyn would never want to be "cured". They loved what they did, and so the only reason they'd look for such a place would be to destroy it if they could, just to get rid of the risk that anybody else might find it and use it against them.

It didn't seem very likely to me that anybody ever would, but I guess you never know. Daniel had to have found out all this stuff from somewhere, and if he could find out then maybe somebody else could too. And then of course they were all tied up in knots about me or Cameron finding it first, because of that stupid old prophecy. In their eyes it was nothing but a danger that needed to be wiped out as soon as possible.

But it made me think, you know. If the water from the sweet spring could really break the curse, then maybe, just maybe. . .

See what I mean about how hope will make a fool of you if you don't watch it? As soon as that tiny little hope slipped into my head, I almost instantly got sucked into a much bigger and wilder and crazier hope, that I could somehow have my family back. It was so sharp and keen it almost physically hurt, even after all this time. But reality is a stubborn thing, and I quickly slammed a lid down on that kind of thinking. Mama and Daddy would hate me if I tried to cure them, whether it worked or not. I knew that just as sure as I knew anything, and that was a project I wasn't going to touch with a ten foot pole.

I could see how they might think I would, though. Especially since I fit the description of the Curse-Breaker. None of that stuff was written in the journal (unless it was in one of the sections I couldn't read), but of course that's the kind of short and easy thing people wouldn't have much trouble passing along by word of mouth. Seventh-generation boy with blue eyes is dangerous. How hard is that to remember? It all made sense, in a depressing kind of way.

I couldn't help wondering if that's why they always seemed like they didn't really want me when I was a kid. I never could understand that before and I always used to wonder what was wrong with me. Maybe I'll never know for sure, but I was willing to lay a pretty good bet on it.

Chapter Six

I shut the book and sat there moodily for a while. I understood now why they spent so much time and effort to find me, because of the prophecy. But it also seemed like one of those self-fulfilling kinds of things that only come true because you think they will. If they'd left me alone and let me go then the chances were a thousand to one that I never would have even heard about any of this stuff. If they'd left Cameron alone and just made him a *loup-garou* when his time came, he probably never would have thought twice about it. It was by pushing too hard and trying to take things into their own hands that they were causing all this stuff to happen.

It was maddening in a way. I hadn't asked for any of this. All I wanted was to be left alone, and then I had to have this big messy problem dumped in my lap. Why me?

I think I was asking that question of God more than anybody else. I knew why the wolves wouldn't leave me alone. That was understandable now. But why did it have to happen at all? That's what I kept wanting to chew on, and I think the more I found out the less I understood and the angrier I got.

"We don't always have to understand everything, Zach," Justin said. I guess he knew what I was thinking from the look on my face, or something like that. Sometimes I feel like Justin should have been a counselor or a psychiatrist instead of a scientist.

"Why me, though? I don't want to deal with any of this," I said. I knew he could hear the anger in my voice, but at that point I didn't care. I had good reason to be mad at all these people for putting me through this. Justin ignored my bad mood, though.

"Do you remember last spring, when you found the puppy in the road on the way home from school?" he asked.

The question mystified me.

"Yeah, sure, I remember. What about it?" I asked.

"What did you do with that puppy?" he asked me.

"I brought it home for a few days and kept it in a box on the back porch, till it wandered off again," I said.

"And why did you do that?" he asked.

"Well, because it was hungry and weak and there was nobody else to take care of it. You would have done the same thing," I said.

"It wasn't your problem, though. You didn't ask for a puppy, and you weren't looking for one. It just popped up one day with no warning, didn't it?" he asked.

"Yeah, but. . ." I said. Then I stopped. I saw what he was getting at, well enough; he just wanted me to connect the dots and be the first one to say it out loud. Justin likes to do that, whenever he thinks I need to remember something. He never exactly tells me anything, he just asks questions.

"You're saying just because I didn't ask for something, that doesn't mean it's not still my responsibility. Like the puppy was, after I found it on the road. I saw it was starving and it would have been wrong of me to turn away and not do something about it. Is that it?" I asked him. I was pretty sure that's what he meant.

I didn't like where this was going. I thought I knew what he was trying to get me to say, but that still didn't mean I wanted to hear it.

"Exactly! And what's that got to do with what's happening now?" he went on.

"You mean I should do whatever I can to fix this problem, even though I didn't ask for it," I said dully. I knew he was right, but that didn't make it any better. If he was any other man I would have been mad at him too, for making me see what I didn't want to see.

He still wasn't done with me, though.

"Zach, do I love you?" he asked me. That was another question I wasn't expecting, but I knew the answer to that one, too, and it softened my mood to remember it.

"Yes, you do. You love me more than anybody else in the world does," I said.

"Yeah I do, and don't you ever forget it. You're the best thing God ever gave me. But if you'll think back just a little bit, you might remember a little boy who showed up on my doorstep one day with nowhere to go, who I didn't ask for and sure wasn't expecting. . . " he went on. He left it hanging there, just like that, but I was starting to catch the drift by then.

"I know what you want me to say, Justin. You want me to tell you that sooner or later we always end up being glad we did the right thing, even when it's something we didn't expect and didn't want to have to do," I said. He nodded.

"Yeah, but it's not even just that. I think this is something you're meant to do, Zach. I believe you really *are* the Curse-Breaker, the one who has a chance to end this evil thing. That's not a burden, kid. It's a chance to do a good thing which nobody else in the world could do. Don't turn away from that. When it's all said and done, I think you'll be glad," he said.

I wanted to ask him about what Mama and Daddy would think of me if I did such a thing and how I was supposed to ever feel glad about *that,* but I couldn't do it with Cameron there. There are certain things you can only talk about in private, and that was *definitely* one of them.

But nevertheless, Justin had a point, and it was a hard one. He was telling me in other words that all things work together for good to those who love God, which was one of his favorite Scripture verses. He believed it to the core of his being, but the question was, did *I* believe it? Oh, I would have *said* I did, if anybody had asked me. But when push came right down to shove and I had to put my money where my mouth was, that was a whole 'nother thing. Did I really believe I'd end up being glad someday that I did the right thing, even if Mama and Daddy hated me for it? I could maybe understand accepting it or thinking it was necessary for me to do it, but the being glad part was hard to swallow.

I was full of doubts, and it was downright terrifying to think about trusting an old promise that much, even one from God. I was ashamed of myself for thinking like that, but I won't pretend I didn't. All I can say is that sometimes the world seems very real and the stuff you learn in church seems very faint and far away.

Justin was watching me, and maybe he knew what I was feeling.

"Don't say anything right now. Just think about it awhile," he said.

I struggled with it most of the way home, and didn't come one single millimeter closer to figuring out how I felt. It was a lot thornier problem than you might think. It's true that I ran away from home to keep from being cursed, and it was also true that my family wouldn't have anything to do with me after that, but somewhere in the back of my mind I always believed there was a chance they might forgive me and we could all be close again, even if we disagreed about the werewolf thing. You hear about stuff like that all the time. It might not even happen till I was grown up, but there was always the chance.

But if I took it upon myself to try to break the curse for good, then that would be the end of it. They'd never forgive me for that, ever. There was no way I could fool myself about that.

I'm not sure what it was that made me decide to trust the promise. Maybe it was that story Justin told me about when I first came to live with him, or maybe it was something else. Maybe when it's all said and done, you can only say that you are what you do.

I decided that I'd go along with it, at least for now. I could see what it took, and I could always change my mind later if I wanted to. It wasn't much trust, I know, but right then it was all I had.

I was still uneasy and troubled inside, but I have to say I felt much better for making some kind of a decision.

All the same, I decided not to think about it anymore for a while. It was much better to focus on making plans than it was to tear myself to pieces over whether I could handle it or not.

Then I had an afterthought. Daddy had told me once that it wasn't possible to ever cure somebody who became a *loup-garou*. That might have been a lie, of course, but it made me wonder. What could breaking the curse mean, if it wasn't that?

I turned halfway around in my seat.

"Cameron, what exactly does it mean when it talks about breaking the curse? Daddy always told me you couldn't cure somebody once they became a *loup-garou*," I asked. Cameron shrugged.

"Yeah, I always heard that, too. I don't know, Zach. Nobody ever told me what it meant," he admitted.

I mulled that over for a while and started to wonder if maybe it was talking about the flat rocks where people had to go to become werewolves. Those might be cursed places. Maybe the water destroyed them and made it so they couldn't be used for that purpose anymore.

That was several "ifs" and "maybes" too many, of course, but the idea had one really good piece of evidence to back it up. It would be something so terrible (for the wolves) that it would be worth all the time and effort they were spending to try to find the spring and destroy it. It was a threat to everything they cared about. A person who was cured could always be cursed again, probably, but a stone which was cleansed. . . that was forever. Nothing in the journal talked about making new stones, just using the ones that happened to be there.

I just hoped I was right.

"I think I know the answer," I finally said.

"Yeah?" Justin asked.

"Yeah. I don't think the spring will cure anybody who's already a werewolf; me and Cameron both heard that from different people, so it's probably true. So the only thing I can think of is that the water will break the curse on the places where people go to become wolves in the first place. We've got maps of where they all are, so all we need to do is find the spring and go break the curses," I explained. It sounded simple, when I put it that way.

"We don't know for sure that you're right, though. It might not work," Justin pointed out.

"Well, no, but I can't think of anything else it might mean. I think we should give it a try, at least," I said.

I was sure that was the right thing to do, and I was sure that's what Justin thought, too, in his heart of hearts. But he also worries about me, and I guess that thought had been bubbling up in his mind while we talked.

"That's a lot of guesswork, Zach, and dealing with these people can be dangerous, especially if they start thinking you're really trying to break the curse. There's no telling what they might do," he reminded me.

"Besides that," he went on, "we still have to find the place. How would you know when you found the right spring?"

I have to confess, that one stumped me. I hadn't thought about that aspect of it at all.

I opened up the notebook again and read over a few of the entries about various springs they had tested. And you know, it never did say anything about what they were testing for or how they knew when they found the right one or not. It just described the location on the map and said it wasn't the right spring, with no more details. That could be a problem.

"Well, it says it's the sweet spring. Maybe it tastes sweet when you drink it," I suggested. Justin smiled a little.

"It'd be nice if it was that easy, but I think we ought to have something a little more solid to work with than that, Zach," he told me.

"Then we need to find out. Somebody has to know something," I said. He shook his head in an I-don't-know kind of way and shrugged.

That was all we said about it for a while. I was tired from so much running and thinking, and I leaned the seat back a little bit to close my eyes and maybe take a snooze the rest of the way home. I could figure out what to do next after that.

I think I actually went to sleep for a while, because the next thing I knew we were pulling up in the driveway at home. There are a couple of potholes in the drive that always make you feel like you're about to bust a tire when you hit them, and that's what woke me up. I don't think I've ever been so glad to see the place.

Eileen was still in Houston, so there was nobody else who needed to fuss over me right then. Which was good, because I needed to think. Justin unlocked the front door for us, and then pulled out his phone and called Eileen to let her know we made it home okay. It wasn't long before they got to talking about other things, so he was busy for a little while.

"Come on, Cameron. Let's see if we can figure this thing out," I said.

We went to my room and laid the journal and the notebook and the section maps on my desktop, and then I turned on my computer. We had a lot of research to do and I figured we better get with it.

So that's what we did for the rest of the afternoon. I love the Internet as much as anybody else does, but sometimes I wish you didn't have to wade through so much junk to find what you're looking for.

What I was looking for was stuff about werewolves. I already knew a good bit about the subject, of course, but the journal was chock full of things I wanted to find out more about. You never want to go off half-cocked and do something serious without knowing what you're dealing with first. That's how people make stupid mistakes.

Anyway, there was no shortage of information about werewolves; where they came from, what they were, what to feed one; you name it, somebody had a website about it. Most of it was stupid stuff, but we couldn't afford to give up looking.

We found several real-life stories of people who claimed to have seen werewolves, and I noticed that some of them were from places close to where the stones in the journal were. We found one story by a woman in Greggton, Texas, and I paid particular attention to that one. It didn't say a whole lot, just that a hairy man-shaped thing came up to her bedroom window one night and nearly scared her to death, and then nosed around her barn yard in the moonlight for a while before it disappeared into the woods.

It doesn't sound like much of a story, but the fact that it happened in Greggton was enough to make me believe it might be true. I saved that one to look at some more later.

There were plenty of other stories from places that were nowhere near any of the stones, of course, but I tried to at least skim all of them. I didn't want to overlook anything important.

I read for hours, until my eyes started to get grainy and my head hurt from looking at the screen so long. When I couldn't handle it anymore then Cameron took a turn for a while.

We didn't just read stories, though. One of the first things we did was to find a list of every place in North America which is called Wolf Mountain. That part wasn't as hard as I thought it would be. The U.S. Geological Survey keeps maps of everything from Tennessee to Timbuktu, and all the names on all the maps are indexed. All you have to do is search the database for a name and leave everything else blank, and it pulls up a list for you, just as pretty as you please. I wish everything could be that easy.

Unfortunately, there are a *lot* of places named Wolf Mountain. Hundreds of them, in fact. That list must have gone on for miles.

At first I was discouraged when I saw how many of them there were. There was no possible way we could look at that many mountains. It would take a million years. No wonder the wolves hadn't been able to find the right place yet.

"I've seen this list before, I think," Cameron said.

"Yeah?" I asked.

"Yeah, my mom has one like it. I think they already checked all the ones in Alabama and most of Tennessee now, and part of Missouri and Arkansas. It just takes forever," he told me.

I had no trouble at all believing that, but I meant to go about it smarter than they did.

"There's got to be some way to figure out which one is the right place, or at least narrow it down a little," I said, half to myself.

"I don't know about that, Zach. Nobody else has ever been able to find anything," he pointed out.

"Well. . . let's look at the map again," I suggested.

I opened the journal to look at that smudgy last page again. I didn't know what I was looking for, really, just hoping we might have overlooked something.

There was a scrawl of numbers at the bottom corner of the page, but I couldn't tell for sure what they were because of the fire damage. You could also see where there used to be some other features marked, here and there; you just couldn't read them. In fact, it looked almost like somebody had tried to wipe out the map on purpose so no one could use it anymore.

There was no telling about something like that, of course, and maybe I was imagining things because I still wanted to believe somebody in my family tried to do the right thing at some point. Wishful thinking again, most likely. Like I said before, hope will sneak up and bite you on the foot when you least expect it, if you don't watch yourself.

I finally decided it didn't matter what happened to the map. I didn't need to know how it got so grimy and obscure. What I needed was to figure out a way to read the dadgummed thing.

There was a time when I used to like to read about invisible ink and stuff like that. I think every boy goes through that phase at some time or another when he tries writing notes with lemon juice and all that jazz. I was no different. I lost interest after a while, but I still remembered a few things that might help us.

"Maybe we could find a way to read all this smudgy writing again," I said.

"Like how?" Cameron asked.

"Watch and see," I told him.

Have you ever noticed when you write with a pencil or a pen, how the point pushes down into the paper and leaves an imprint of the letters? I bet you never thought about that, did you? Even if you go back and erase the writing later, the imprint is sometimes still there, and if you're careful (and just a little bit lucky) you can sometimes decipher old writing that way. I remembered that from my invisible ink days.

There are a couple of ways to go about it, but the easiest and quickest way is to use a magnifying glass, the stronger the better. I had one in my desk drawer, and after rummaging around a while I found it. It wasn't the strongest in the world, but maybe it would do.

"I don't think that'll work, dude," Cameron said when he saw it.

"Well. . . it wouldn't hurt to give it a try, would it?" I asked him. He just shrugged again and didn't say anything.

I laid the journal open flat on the desktop and turned on my lamp so it shined down directly on the paper, then I got to work.

The first thing I had to do was see if there was anything to work with. It only took me a few seconds to see the faint grooves made by the pencil. They were barely visible, but there they were.

"That won't work, Zach. Mama already tried that several times. Nobody could ever read anything that way," Cameron said again.

I soon discovered he was right. The grooves were too faint for me to do anything with them. The writing was just too old, and that fancy curly-cue script didn't help either. I could see it was there, but I couldn't make out what it said. That was frustrating.

"I think it's time to try something more drastic," I suggested.

Even though I couldn't read the grooves by themselves, I might be able to do it if I filled them in again. That was a risky plan since I might wreck my only clue, but they say fortune favors the bold. If the wolves had ever thought of trying something like that, they obviously never had the guts to actually go for it and mark in the book.

"I think I'll try to trace over those grooves with a sharp pencil, so maybe we can see them better," I said.

I got a new pencil and sharpened it to the sharpest point I possibly could without breaking it.

"Here, hold the magnifying glass for me," I said to Cameron. He took it and held it as steady as he could, so I could concentrate on the paper. Then, being as careful as if I was handling precious jewels, I used the point of my pencil to lightly fill in those old writing grooves.

A lot of them were impossible to follow, and I didn't dare try to guess. I stuck strictly to what I saw, and nothing more.

It was the kind of tiny, careful work that makes your hand hurt after a while, and by the time I finished the results didn't look like much. I still couldn't be completely sure what it said, but with a little guesswork I thought I could read parts of it now.

There was what looked like a stream or a road marked on the map, and next to it was the word "Coe." There was another word after that which I couldn't read, but I thought it might be "creek." I wasn't sure about that part, though.

I thought I could make out the name of another mountain to the northeast, but even with my best efforts I couldn't read any more than the first letter, which seemed to be *K*.

I couldn't read anything else on the map no matter how hard I tried.

It might sound like awfully nitpicky results, after all the work we had to put in. But I hoped it might be enough. Out of all the Wolf Mountains, surely there couldn't be that many of them with a Coe something-or-other nearby and another mountain whose name started with K.

That called for some more searching on the USGS site. Turns out there are quite a few Coe Creeks, too. Not to mention Coe Trails, Coe Roads, and Coe Bluffs. That was okay, though, because I had a trick up my sleeve to deal with that. One thing I like about the USGS site is that it gives latitude and longitude coordinates for every feature. I imported the list of Wolf Mountains into a spreadsheet and then imported the Coe-thing list and cross-referenced the two collections by latitude and longitude so I could see if any of them were close to each other.

It took quite a bit of time to do all that, but after I crunched the data, I found out there's only one Wolf Mountain with a Coe Creek nearby. They both matched up at 33 degrees North, 93 degrees West, and when I checked the minutes and seconds those lined up too.

"Perfect match," I said with satisfaction.

I have to admit I was a little smug about the whole thing and patted myself on the back a few times. I was ninety-nine percent sure I knew the exact spot the wolves were looking for, when none of them had been able to figure it out. I let myself feel good about that for a few minutes.

Anyway, I went to another part of the site and pulled a map for those coordinates, and that's when I got a shock. That particular Wolf Mountain was less than four miles from my house. That was hard to believe, and almost creepy in a way.

Justin always says nothing happens by accident. You may never know the reason for something, but that doesn't mean there's not one. I thought about what he said earlier on the way home, about how he thought I was the Curse-Breaker, and I wondered if finding the mountain so close to us meant anything.

Chapter Seven

For a while I wanted to lay it off on other things. I hadn't known a thing about that mountain before I came here, and I was sure Justin and Eileen didn't either. They moved to Texarkana for reasons that had nothing to do with the mountain, or even with me. I was just along for the ride wherever Justin went.

It had to be a complete accident, unless somebody had it all planned out and it was somehow meant to be that way. There were no other ways I could think of to explain it, and I wasn't sure I liked either one.

After a while I decided it didn't matter which it was. The spring was right in my back yard, and that was a good thing, and if I was as smart as the average doorknob I wouldn't look a gift horse in the mouth. I'd reach out and take it.

I still wasn't sure exactly where the Sweet Spring might be or how we'd recognize it when we found it. But at least we knew where to look, and that was more than the wolves had.

On the other hand, they did have that list of all the places named Wolf Mountain, and they knew where I lived. It might not have crossed their minds to compare the two things yet, but sooner or later it would. As soon as that happened, they'd be out there on that mountain like a duck on a June bug. The fact that it was so close to me would be enough to put it right up at the top of their list. It wouldn't matter whether they could read the map from the journal or not. They'd guess, and this time they'd hit the bull's eye.

If they hadn't already.

I glanced at my window, where the daylight was fading fast. It was too late to go out and explore the place tonight. It would be a lot better to head out there early in the morning and have the whole day to nose around. It would probably take at least a whole day, and maybe more.

"I think we need to go out there and look for the spring right away," I said, and Cameron nodded.

I printed a copy of the topographical map just so we'd have it handy the next morning, and laid it aside so it wouldn't get lost in the meantime.

"You know they might show up while we're out there in the woods. What do we do then?" Cameron pointed out.

"That's a nasty idea. But we've got silver if it comes to that," I told him. I reached up and showed him my silver cross. Justin had found it down by the lakeshore when he got in from Houston, and he set it on my desktop to wait for me.

"This is sharp on the ends. It's the best weapon I could have," I said confidently. Then I opened my desk drawer and pulled out an old nail file. It had silver tips on both ends, and one of the tips was sharp enough to break skin if need be. It's what I used to carry around with me until I got the cross.

"Here, take this with you. It's sharp and it's silver, and that's all you need," I told him. Cameron took the nail file and slipped it in his pocket.

"Yeah, but what about Logan? Silver won't work on him, yet," he reminded me.

"There's nothing we can do about that except run away if we see him," I said.

"Well you can't miss him. He's got the hairiest hands and arms you ever saw. He looks like Bigfoot in cowboy boots," Cameron said.

"Yeah, I'll remember that," I said dryly.

* * * * * * *

The next morning we got up at the crack of dawn and headed out to the mountain with Justin.

It turned out that "mountain" was a really generous word for the place. It was more like a mole-hill than a mountain, to my way of thinking. It was nothing compared to the Smokies, or even the Ozarks. Still, it was the highest point anywhere close by and it *was* fairly steep in places, so I decided not to quibble about the name.

Justin parked the truck on the side of a gravel road at the foot of the place, and then we started searching.

It turns out there are several springs on Wolf Mountain, as a matter of fact. We found that out the hard way, by walking all the way around the dadgummed thing. Me and Justin and Cameron all split up and started walking around the base of it, since we could cover more ground faster that way. We took backpacks and a bunch of empty plastic bottles to fill up with water just in case we found the spring. Whoever found it first was supposed to head back to the truck and call the others so we didn't waste any more time.

Since we didn't know exactly what we were looking for, we were supposed to fill up a bottle from every spring we found, just in case. We all took a permanent marker with us so we could mark each bottle according to where it came from.

It wasn't too hard of a job. Every time I crossed a little creek bed I turned and followed it upstream to the source, somewhere up on the hillside. More often than not it petered out in a dry wash that only carried rain water and didn't really amount to much. Then I had to walk all the way back down to the base and move on to the next one. I can't even count how many of those piddly little things there were, but I didn't dare overlook one.

I found the Sweet Spring itself about mid-afternoon, and it was the third one I looked at. It felt hot enough to fry eggs on the rocks by then, although I guess that's partly because I was working so hard climbing.

I'd been going up a fairly steep gully on the northwest side of the hill, and the sun was beating down on me like a hammer the whole time. I was sweating buckets and breathing a little hard, and I had a pounding headache from the heat.

That's when I found the spring. The gully made a sudden sharp turn to the right, and there it was.

It wasn't much of one, as springs go. Just a slow, steady drip from an overhanging cliff wall, which formed a pool about the size of a mixing bowl before it dried up or sank into the ground or whatever it did.

None of that was very interesting, but then I noticed that somebody had carved words into the soft sandstone above the dripping water. I didn't see them at first because I wasn't paying attention to that area, but when I did glance up, there they were. Whoever carved them must have spent days and days to finish, because the letters were deep. They looked old and weathered, like they'd been there for a hundred years, but they were still easy to read. They said *To make broken things whole.*

Whatever that was supposed to mean.

There was nothing else to see, and I was incredibly thirsty by then, so I got down on my knees and took a sip.

The water was clear and cold, just like I like it, but it also tasted faintly sweet, like somebody had dumped a spoonful of sugar in it. I swallowed, and then I took another drink. This time I swished it around in my mouth for a minute, and I decided it didn't taste quite like sugar water. There was something else about it, too. It was more like the nectar you taste when you bite the tip off a honeysuckle blossom, except that's only a tiny little drop and this was a whole mouthful.

It had to be the right place.

I wanted to dance or sing or do something to show how excited I was, but I contained myself. I just opened a plastic bottle and carefully filled it up from the bowl, then screwed the lid on tight so it wouldn't leak. I marked the bottle with a big X, and then stuck it in my backpack. Then I filled up two more bottles, and that just about emptied the pool. It would take a while for that slow drip to refill it.

If I'd been paying attention, I might have noticed that my headache was gone and I didn't feel sun-sick anymore, but I didn't think about that till later.

At that point I was so pleased with myself that I wasn't thinking about much of anything else, and that was dumb.

I started easing my way back down the gully, pulling out my phone as I went.

I texted Justin and told him I'd found the spring and that I was headed back to the truck. It was a cheap phone and I didn't like it much, but I'd probably have to wait till Christmas before I got a nicer one. I missed my old one that got drowned in the river.

I slipped it back in my pocket without waiting for him to answer; I'd see him soon enough anyway.

I'm usually surefooted as a billy goat, but maybe what happened next was meant to be. A loose rock gave way under my foot and went tumbling down the slope, and the tree branch I grabbed to steady myself broke off at the same time. My body fell backwards after the stone, and I remember thinking maybe I should have been more careful. It's amazing what stupid thoughts go through your head at times like that, isn't it?

A second later I felt a crushing blow on my right side when I hit one of the boulders not far below me. That's the last thing I remember.

When I opened my eyes, I was lying at the bottom of the steepest part of the gully, and the spot I fell from must have been at least twenty feet up. The sun hadn't moved from where it was, so I couldn't have been out for long. I guess I must have hit my head on something, although I didn't remember it. There was some matted blood in my hair and I had a splitting headache.

I tried to sit up and almost didn't make it. My right side was killing me, and I gritted my teeth from the pain. I felt like I'd been run over by a steamroller. It even hurt to breathe. I found bruises and cuts on my face and all over my body, and I could almost swear I had a broken rib or two. It felt like it anyway.

The pain in my head kept me from thinking as clearly as I usually would have, but after a while I remembered my cell phone. I had no idea what part of the mountain Justin was on or how far he might have to walk to get to me, but I seriously doubted I could move at all.

I got the phone out of my pocket, and that's when I saw that the sharp point of a rock had smashed the screen sometime when I fell. It wouldn't even come on. I was getting to be an expert at destroying phones, it seemed.

Well, I'd just have to wait. Justin knew where I was, sort of, and when I didn't show up at the truck he'd come looking for me after a while to see what happened. It might be a few hours, but I could tough it out that long if I had to.

I tried to move into the shade so the sun wasn't hitting me dead on, but it hurt so much it brought tears to my eyes and I had to stop. It takes a lot of pain to make me cry, but this was bad enough to do it.

So I laid there and felt sorry for myself for a while and wondered if I'd die before anybody found me. You hear about things like that, you know. I didn't know if I was hurt that bad or not, but it sure did feel like it.

My tongue felt like a piece of leather in my mouth, so I took a drink from one of the bottles. It was one of the ones that had sweet water in it, but at the time I couldn't have cared less about wasting it. We could always go back and get more.

Not long after I swallowed the water, I stopped hurting. I couldn't help but notice *that,* and within a minute or so I felt like nothing had ever happened.

My ribs didn't hurt, my head didn't hurt, and when I looked down at my body there wasn't a mark or a scratch on it anywhere. There were a couple of rips and some blood on my clothes, but that was all.

I had a weird sense of unreality wash over me. Did I fall down the rocks or not? They say when you have to ask yourself if you're crazy then you're probably not, so I decided it must have really happened.

Then I remembered those words I found carved on the stone: *To make broken things whole.* Well, I was certainly broken, and after I drank the water I was whole again. That fit well enough.

Except I never had a clue the water could do such a thing. I thought it was just for getting rid of curses, because that's what it said in the journal. But then again, maybe the wolves didn't know half as much about it as they thought they did.

When I got to thinking about it, I decided after a while that a curse was a kind of brokenness, too. It was something wrong and twisted in the world. So the water should make that kind of thing whole again, too, shouldn't it? Maybe the stone could just as well have said *"To make twisted things straight,"* or even *"To make wrong things right."*

I looked at the bottle in my hand with something like awe. In fact it *still* awes me when I think about it, even now when I'm writing this. Even after everything we found out later and all the stuff that happened, it doesn't knock the shine off it at all. When you come face to face with a miracle, you never forget it.

After a few minutes I got up and started walking back down to where the truck was parked, still too amazed to think of anything else.

Justin and Cameron weren't there yet, so I opened the passenger side door and got in to wait for them.

Justin came walking up to the truck not too long after that, looking tired but kinda happy.

At least until he got to the truck, that is. I still had blood on my clothes and in my hair and I must have looked worse than I thought, because his jaw dropped when he saw me. He was beside me before a cat could lick its tail.

"What happened?" he gasped.

"Uh, I fell down some rocks, but it's okay," I said.

"How bad are you hurt?" he asked.

"I'm fine. Really," I told him. He didn't look like he believed me, but I guess he saw there was no fresh blood and maybe that made him feel a little better about things.

"Don't worry, bubba. We'll take you down to the hospital and get you all fixed up," he told me.

"I really think I could just go home and rest, Justin. I'll be fine," I told him again, but he wouldn't hear of the idea.

"No, Zach. I want somebody to check you out first, just to be safe. You may have hurt yourself worse than you think," he told me. I didn't think there was any need, but I went ahead to the emergency room to have them look me over.

The nurse saw the blood all over and hurried me inside right away, and then she carefully felt my head for cuts. She couldn't find any, so she washed the blood out of my hair with some warm water so she could see better. She still couldn't find anything, so she told me to go home and rest, and to call if I felt worse during the night.

Justin didn't say much on the way home that day, and I wasn't all that anxious to talk anyway. I had a lot to think about.

When we got home I laid down on the couch and watched TV for a few hours and stayed awake like they told me I should, and then when nothing happened I went to bed.

Justin went back out to the mountain to get Cameron at some point, but I don't remember exactly when.

In the morning I got up quietly and looked at myself in the mirror. There wasn't a scratch to see, and I wondered all over again if the whole accident had been nothing but a vivid dream. I might even have convinced myself that's what it was, if I hadn't seen my torn and bloody clothes from yesterday in the laundry basket. Those were too real to ignore.

I padded into the kitchen to scrounge up something for breakfast, still lost in thought. Eileen was sitting at the table having a cup of coffee; I guess she must have got home from Houston sometime late last night after I was already in bed. She had her hair tied up in a bun and didn't really look like herself that way. She's much prettier with it down.

Anyway, she always says not to talk to her in the morning until after her second cup of coffee, even if you're dying, so I didn't say anything. Justin and Cameron were still asleep, I guessed.

"I thought you hurt yourself yesterday, Zach," she said, looking me up and down. She must have already had her second cup this morning.

"Yeah, I fell down some rocks. It wasn't too bad. I'm okay," I told her, shrugging. She raised one eyebrow at me.

"That's not what I heard last night. Justin said there was blood all over you when he found you," she said. There was no denying it, so I didn't try.

"Yeah, there was," I said. It wasn't that I wanted to hide anything from her; it's just that I still didn't know what to think about it. It all seemed so unreal again today.

"I saw your clothes, Zach, and I heard what Justin said and what the nurse at the hospital told him yesterday. And now I see you walking around without a scratch on you this morning. You don't think that's strange?" she asked, mildly.

"Well, yeah, but I don't know what to say. It's weird. I can't explain it," I told her. She smiled a little.

"Aw, it's a totally different thing to not be able to explain something. I see things in the lab all the time that I can't explain. But that's when you need to keep your eyes open the most, and not just pretend it's not there or it didn't happen. That's how you find out things," she said. It was exactly the kind of thing I would have expected her to say.

"So what happened yesterday?" she went on. I decided it couldn't hurt to get her opinion. She already knew about the journal and the topographical maps and what we'd been searching for yesterday, so there was no need to repeat all that.

"I found the Sweet Spring yesterday, Eileen," I told her.

"Yeah, Justin told me that's what you said. But how do you know for sure?" she asked.

"Partly because the water tasted sweet, like honeysuckle nectar. And then also because there was a rock face above it where somebody carved the words *To make broken things whole.* Those two things together made me pretty sure it was the right place as soon as I found it. But there's more, too," I told her.

"Yeah, I thought there might be. So what happened next?" she asked.

"I filled up some bottles with as much water as I could, and then I headed back down. But I slipped on a loose rock and fell maybe twenty feet and hit something. When I woke up there was blood everywhere and I hurt so much I couldn't move. I was thirsty from lying in the hot sun, so I took another drink of sweet water from one of the bottles I had with me. Then all of a sudden I felt fine. Not a scratch on me," I told her.

"So yesterday you were covered with cuts and bruises, you lost a lot of blood, and you were in pretty bad pain, right?" she asked.

"Yeah, you could say that," I said dryly.

"But after you drank the water you're not even scratched," she said.

"Not as far as I can tell. It's almost like it never happened," I admitted.

"Did you do anything else unusual yesterday that might account for that fact, other than drink that water?" she asked.

"Not that I can think of," I said.

"Then for now the logical answer is that the water from the spring made you whole, just like it said on the stone," she said calmly, like it was the most ordinary thing in the world.

"But how could that be?" I asked.

"I don't pretend to know how it could be. But I see the evidence right in front of my eyes, and I'm not inclined to doubt it. We already knew the water was special, if it cures curses. We just didn't know how special it really was," she pointed out.

Eileen is so utterly reasonable sometimes. I wonder if she ever has an illogical thought in her head. It was hard to disagree with her once she laid it all out for me like that. Maybe that's what I needed to hear before I could totally believe it myself. If Eileen could accept it that easily, then I could too. I smiled a little.

"Thanks, Eileen," I told her. She smiled back and patted my hand.

"Anytime, champ," she said.

I was about to say something else when Justin walked into the room. He was still sleepy and looked like it, but he saw us at the kitchen table and came to sit down with us.

"I think we need to find out a lot more about that spring, babe," Eileen told him before he could say anything.

"Yeah? Why's that?" he asked.

"Well, from what Zach tells me it sounds like he was hurt pretty bad yesterday, till he drank that water. Then after that he was fine as frog hair, it seems. If the spring can do things like that, then I think we need to find out what all it *can* do," she said. Justin nodded.

"Then I think that should be your project, babe. Good thinkin'," he told her. She gave him one of those smiles that make you embarrassed even to watch, and I wanted to disappear into my chair. It's always like that when they get all mushy with each other that way. I felt like it was high time to change the subject.

"Okay, we've got the water from the spring, and we know where the cursed stones are. I think we should go try to destroy them while we still can," I finally said. I was a lot more interested in breaking curses than I was in satisfying my curiosity, at least for now. That could wait till later.

"We still don't know for sure that you're right about that, Zach," Justin pointed out, "But still, it *is* something we need to find out one way or the other as soon as we can. The stone in Greggton is the closest one, I think. We should probably go down there first and see what happens. Make sure it works before we go too far out on a limb."

"Yeah, I think that would be the best thing," I agreed, nodding.

"Okay then. There's no time like the present, so let's get dressed and get going. Go wake up Cameron and get everything together. We've got a long way ahead of us," he said.

Chapter Eight

It's not really all that far to Longview from where we live in Texarkana. A couple hours maybe, if you take your time. Greggton, where the stone was located, is on the west side of town.

We got there while it was still early, and followed the map in the journal out to a farm on Swinging Bridge Road.

It was strange, actually. Most of the area around there was built up with new houses and suburbs and stuff, but here was this big chunk of land with a faded red barn and an old farmhouse sitting at the edge of it, grown up in slash pine and scrub oak and sweet gum saplings and patches of weedy pasture. It looked like nobody had lived there in a thousand years.

Well maybe not quite that long, but you know what I mean.

On the other hand, there was a metal gate across the lane that led up to the house, and a bright red "No Trespassing" sign which clearly wasn't very old at all. That made me uneasy. Somebody was watching the place at least now and then.

I hadn't brought the journal with me. I didn't think it was safe to take it somewhere like that, where it might fall back into the hands of the wolves. What I did instead was make a copy of the map for this place, and I had that with me. The journal itself I hid in the barn at home under a pile of ropes in the hay loft where I keep the extra tack. Nobody would find it out there.

Justin had a silver dagger that he bought at a tattoo shop downtown, and me and Cameron had one too. They were stupid looking things with pewter handles in the shape of dragons, and they had pink rhinestone eyes. Made to hang on the wall and look pretty, no doubt, not really to use. But the blades were plated with real silver, and that was all that mattered. Eileen had a pistol and a box of silver-tipped bullets, so she was in better shape than any of us.

I had a bottle of the sweet water in my pocket so I'd have it ready. The other two bottles were hidden at home in the barn along with the journal, just in case something went wrong.

Eileen killed the truck, and everything was quiet as a mouse on a feather bed. It seemed almost spooky quiet, in fact, but maybe I was just imagining things. There was nothing stopping us from going ahead, but nobody seemed anxious to get started.

"All right, let's do this," I finally said.

That got everybody in motion. Justin got out, and me and Cameron followed him. Eileen's job was to stay with the truck and pretend she was lost in case anybody showed up, and to either fire the gun or honk the horn or something like that so we'd know to get the heck out of there if we had to. Girls can get away with that kind of thing easier than guys can, you know. We were hoping nobody would show up at all, but if they did then she could handle them.

The map from the journal showed a little creek flowing back behind the barn, and the rock was supposed to be on a low bluff overlooking that creek. It didn't look too hard to find. With a little luck, we could be in and out fast.

I climbed the gate and jumped down on the other side, and Justin and Cameron came after me a bit slower.

The lane on the other side was dusty and weedy, like nobody ever used it much. We walked in the ruts and didn't stop to admire the scenery until we were up behind the ramshackle old barn and somewhat hidden from prying eyes. Then we stopped to look at the map again.

"Can you tell which way to go from here?" Justin whispered. I don't know why he was whispering, actually, but the silence of the place didn't seem to like being broken.

The barn was clearly marked on the map, and the creek was supposed to be somewhere to the east. I couldn't see it because of the saplings and undergrowth, but it had to be there. It looked like the easiest thing to do would be to walk directly east until we came to the water, then turn and walk south till we reached the bluff where the stone was supposed to be. That way we wouldn't get lost in the woods.

The barn itself was on a slight rise in the ground, so we started going downhill almost immediately. Most of that area was a thicket of slash pines maybe ten feet tall. They grew so close together we had to elbow our way through them in places. We could have brought a machete and had an easier time of it, probably, but I really didn't want to leave any signs that we'd been there if I could help it. It would be hard for anybody to miss a machete trail.

It wasn't too far to the creek, as it turned out. In fact the main reason we found it is because we nearly fell in. The pine thicket grew so close to the water that we couldn't see how weak and undercut the bank was in that place. Justin had to grab a tree to keep from falling in when a big chunk of ground collapsed right under his feet, and Cameron had to throw himself backwards. The dirt made a huge splash in the water when it hit.

"That was a close one," I laughed, trying to lighten the tension a little bit. It was thick as curdled cream in the air, and we all felt it.

"Yeah, nearly went for a swim," Justin said, without much humor. Cameron got up and brushed the dirt and pine straw off his back, without saying anything at all. I noticed he kept one hand on a tree branch after that.

The weak spot in the bank didn't go on for long, but even after that there were scads of saw briers close to the water which made it impossible to walk along the shore, so we had to go back to the edge of the pine thicket and struggle our way through that for a while longer.

But by and by the pines thinned out when we started going uphill again, and finally we came to a place where there were mostly big oak trees growing. There was a bluff there, and the creek formed a bend around it. I think the bluff was mostly a rock outcrop, because you could see the stone down near the water level where the creek had washed the dirt away. But none of it showed above ground anywhere else.

Except in one spot.

On the far side of the bluff, in the middle of an oak grove, a single flat tongue of rock poked out of the ground, about three feet high and ten feet long. It had to be the place.

If I hadn't known the secret, I never would have given the rock a second thought, if I ever found it in the first place. It was well hidden, and anybody who stumbled across it by accident would never think it was anything except a flat rock in the woods, just like a million others. But I knew.

We went up to it warily, half expecting somebody to jump out of the woods and catch us there. It wouldn't have surprised me if somebody had. My heart was beating so fast I could feel it in my toes.

But nothing like that happened, and soon we were standing right next to the thing. It was dark charcoal gray, the same color and texture as the one behind my old house in Tennessee. Sandstone, I think, but I wouldn't swear to it. My skin crawled at first, because I knew what this place had been used for. In fact it was *the* stone, the first one, which Daniel had used all those years ago. It was probably the one Mama and Daddy and Nana Maralyn had used, too, come to think of it.

I'm not sure why I was scared. You wouldn't think it would be such a big deal to sprinkle some water on a rock. But I was, though, and my hand shook when I reached for the bottle in my pocket.

Maybe it's because I knew it was my last chance to back out. I could still walk away right then, but after I poured the water on that rock, nothing could ever be the same again. There was no more putting it off, no more time to think it over, and no turning back. I'd be giving up my family forever, and this time it would be my choice and not theirs. That's a lot to ask a kid to do.

Justin noticed, like he notices everything, and put a hand on my shoulder.

"Go ahead, bubba. You can do it," he told me quietly. And you know, that steadied me a little bit. You never feel so afraid as when you're alone, and if somebody who loves you will just stand beside you when the hard time comes, then it makes all the difference in the world. He told me once that no virtue can live when courage is missing, and maybe he was remembering that himself, because courage is what he gave me that day, when I needed it the most.

I made my choice.

I swallowed hard and pulled out the bottle, and started to unscrew the lid. But then I stopped, because something didn't feel quite right.

"Justin, I think we should pray first," I told him. I'm not sure why, really. Sometimes you just feel things, I guess.

"Not a bad idea, but I think you should be the one who does it, Zach," he told me. So I reached out and grasped his hand and Cameron's in mine, and I looked up at the blue sky, and I prayed out loud over that cursed rock, that it should be made whole and clean again. Then I took a deep breath and poured the water on the stone.

I don't know what I expected. Smoke and fire, the rock cracking in two, something dramatic like that.

But all that happened was that the rock turned dark wherever the water touched. I thought at first it was just spots from being wet, and I was disappointed. But then I noticed the spots were getting larger. They grew and grew while I watched, joining together when they got big enough. After a few minutes they were all joined together, and the rock had completely changed color, too. It was reddish brown now, like an ordinary piece of sandstone. I touched it with my finger, and it was warm and wet to the touch, and there was a faint scent of. . . something. I couldn't have said exactly what it was, but it smelled sweet, something like mimosa blossoms in June. I took another deep breath and turned to look at Justin.

"I think we're done here," I told him.

We struggled our way through the pine thicket again and made it back to the truck in record time. It had taken less than an hour to do the whole thing.

We didn't stop to celebrate, though. Eileen put the truck in drive and got us out of there faster than a shopaholic on Dollar Day. She didn't slow down until we were halfway to Marshall.

We stopped at a little greasy spoon restaurant beside the highway to have dinner and talk about things. I sorta like places like that. They always have really good food, and usually they're more interesting than a fast food joint. I ordered a chicken fried steak with mashed potatoes and gravy, and an extra large Dr. Pepper. Breaking curses is thirsty work, you know.

"One down, four to go," I said cheerfully. I felt light-headed and giddy, not at all like I thought I'd feel. I would have thought I'd feel sad or down or some such thing, after what I just did. And maybe I still would, later on, but right then I felt like I was on top of the world. The first place had been wiped out, and I was sure the other ones could be handled just the same way. I was still keyed up and full of energy, or I might not have been so sure of myself.

"I wouldn't be so cocky about it, Zach. That one was easy," Justin warned.

"I wouldn't call it *easy,*" I objected.

"Yeah it was, though. There was no fight, nobody there to defend the place. It's hard for me to believe they'll all be like that. You better wait and see what we're up against before you think it's all over," he insisted.

"Yeah, true, but right now I just want to celebrate what we did this morning. I think it was awesome," I told him. He smiled a little.

"Yeah, I think so too," he admitted.

"Well, if you two are done arguing about that, I think the food is here," Eileen interrupted, with a practical smile.

She was right. The waitress brought our plates and set them down, and I attacked my steak with gusto. There's something about danger that makes you hungry. I don't know what it is, but it's a fact. I didn't stop until the last crumb was gone.

I got a little too full, to tell the truth, and it always makes me sleepy when that happens. I dozed a while in the truck after we left the restaurant, and when we got home I laid down on my bed for a while.

When I woke up it was maybe five o'clock or so. Cameron was nowhere to be seen, but I heard somebody moving around in the kitchen. Justin would have been humming or singing something, so I figured it was Eileen. She likes to cook, and the kitchen is one of her favorite places. Maybe it reminds her of all that sludge and goo she cooks all day at the lab when she's at work.

While I was thinking about that, I spotted a stack of books beside my computer. They hadn't been there earlier, so somebody must have come in and left them there while I was asleep.

I went to see what they were, and found a note sitting on top of the stack.

"Thought these might help out," was all it said, and I recognized Eileen's spidery handwriting. They were library books, so she must have gone to the library and found them for me.

The top one was called *Legends of the Red River Valley,* which I think must have been thick enough to use for a StairMaster. I set it aside and picked up the next one, which was titled *Folklore of Texas.* The others were pretty much the same kind of thing. A bunch of stories and folklore from anywhere near Texarkana.

I was kinda mystified about what all these books were supposed to be good for. Like I said before, history is *not* my most favorite subject, and Eileen knew that. So I was sure she didn't get them for me just for kicks.

But I was down off my high from Greggton by then, and starting to have some of those second thoughts I was afraid I'd end up having, and that wasn't what I wanted to think about right then. I needed something else to keep my mind away from all that, and the books would do.

I picked up *Legends of the Red River Valley* and carried it to the kitchen with me. Sure enough, Eileen was in there baking something. It smelled like barbecued chicken or pork chops or something like that. She looked up when I walked through the door.

"Found your books, I see," she said with a smile.

"Yeah, but what are they for?" I asked her.

"I went to the library this afternoon to see if I could learn anything else about that spring out on the mountain. I figured if there was anything to find, it would be in books like these," she explained.

It made sense, sort of, but I'm not sure I would have thought of it. Eileen is really good about things like that. She's one of the smartest people I ever met, and when she finds something that interests her then she latches on like a pit bull and won't let go till she figures it out. She doesn't get distracted, either. I sometimes think she could be reading an article about organic chemistry in the middle of a war zone and if a bomb exploded next to her she'd just brush the dirt off the page and keep right on studying.

"Don't you ever wonder where it came from and what else it can do and things like that?" she asked.

"Yeah, I guess so," I said, without much enthusiasm. I won't say those kinds of things had never crossed my mind, but right then I was a lot more focused on destroying the stones. But Eileen had taken the trouble to go downtown and find all those books for me, so I felt like I owed it to her to at least pretend I was interested for a while. I didn't have anything else to do at the moment.

I laid the book down on the kitchen table and opened it to the table of contents. The stories were arranged by the date when the compiler had collected each one and the name of the person who told it to him, which wasn't a particularly helpful way of doing it. There were something like five hundred of them in the whole collection.

"You mean I have to read this whole book just on the chance there might be something useful in it somewhere? You've got to be kidding," I said out loud.

"Well, maybe not. Is there an index?" Eileen asked.

"Um, I don't know," I said, embarrassed that I hadn't thought of that. I flipped to the back of the book and there was indeed an index. It didn't seem to be a very good one, but it was better than nothing.

Eileen already had paper and pencil at the table, so I grabbed a sheet and started making notes of any stories that seemed like they might have to do with springs, or werewolves, or anything like that. It was a lot like what I'd been doing searching the Internet, except a lot more time-consuming. Eileen went back to her cooking, and we didn't talk much for a while.

I didn't find anything worth mentioning, just in case you wondered. Just a bunch of old stories that had nothing to do with what I was interested in. I finally shut the cover in disgust after about an hour.

"No luck, huh?" she asked.

"No, just a bunch of old stories about everything in the world except what I want to know," I said.

"Yeah, it happens like that sometimes. Just be patient, Zach," she said.

Eileen was done with the pork chops by then, so she sat down at the table and started skimming through *Legends of the Red River Valley* herself. She didn't bother with the index; just opened the book to page one and started reading. She read at least a little bit of every story, to see if there was anything useful in it. If there wasn't, then she skipped ahead to the next one. She's a fast reader, but as thick as that book was, I still expected it to take her a week to make her way through the whole thing.

I thought she was wasting her time, to be honest. But if she was going to put that much effort into the project, then I felt like I had to do something too. So in spite of my doubts, I picked up *Folklore of Texas* and started to read that one.

After a while I did get mildly interested. The new book wasn't quite so dry and historical as the other one, and it also wasn't near as long. Still nothing useful, though.

Eileen was still wrapped up in her book, so I went back to my room and brought the other ones to the table.

I started on *Tales of the Piney Woods* because it had a nicer cover picture than the other one did. I didn't know any other way to choose between them.

At first I thought Eileen had picked up that one by mistake. It included ten stories written by various people, and it wasn't till I read the fine print on the flyleaf that I noticed they were all adaptations of folk tales from east Texas. Good enough, then.

I enjoyed that one pretty well. It was really just like reading any other story book, and I liked that. The first few stories were fun to read but didn't have anything to do with what I was looking for.

Then I found something.

"Hey, Eileen, listen to this," I said out loud, sitting up straighter in my chair. She looked up from her book.

"What is it, Zach?" she asked.

"This story. You've got to hear it," I said excitedly. Then I started to read aloud.

Chapter Nine

They say this place has always been called Red Lick, even before there was any town here. I don't know if it was named for the river or the dirt, or maybe both, but the deer and the wild animals would always come here and lick the salt from the ground when they needed it.

That meant there was always game to be had, and my grandfather Joram would ride here from his farm down the way, because the hunting was good.

It was the summer of 1863 when he first saw the beast, and he didn't know at first what it was. It was nigh on to evening, and the dark was falling fast. Joram had seen nothing to shoot all day, and he was starting to think it might be best to head home before the night came.

Then he saw a doe standing at the edge of the pine woods, and he stopped to see what she would do. If he could get that deer, it would be well worth riding home in the dark.

The doe raised her ears and stood stock still to listen and smell of the wind, but she was no more still than Joram. He waited patiently until she was satisfied all was safe, and slowly walked into the clearing. She nibbled the dry grass before taking another look around, and then she started to lick the ground where a patch of red clay showed through.

There was a bright full moon at the edge of the sky, and Joram slowly and carefully raised his rifle. The deer was too intent on the salt lick to see him under the shadows of the trees, and he began to hope he had a chance.

Then the beast came. It leapt suddenly out of the darkness of the pine thickets, and fell snarling on the deer before she or Joram had a chance to see it coming. The doe gave a bleat of terror before the beast had her, and that was all.

Joram's heart was beating fast, for the thing was too big for a wolf and not shaped like a mountain lion or anything else he knew. He wanted no part of it, whatever it was, and he began to back slowly away from the scene in hopes it wouldn't notice him.

The moment he moved, the thing stopped eating and raised its head. It cocked one ear to the side, and then looked straight at Joram and gave a low growl.

Now Joram was a brave man, but the vicious beast terrified him, and he forgot everything he knew about the ways of wild animals, and he turned and ran.

The beast didn't follow him. Not that night, and Joram counted himself blessed not to have been killed beside the deer at the salt lick.

Yet he began to notice that all was not well after that day. Cattle and goats disappeared without explanation, and when the moon shone bright in the sky, he often saw large shapes stalking the edges of his pastures at night.

Joram's fear was immense, but he swore to himself to follow the things and make an end, no matter what the danger might be. For if he didn't stop losing his cattle, then his family would starve come winter.

Therefore Joram waited for another night when the moon was full, and the beasts who stalked his land and killed his livestock came again. As always, they slipped away to the east just before sunrise. But this time Joram mounted his steadiest horse and followed behind them.

The things didn't move too fast, and when they crossed the shallows at Cowhorn Creek, he caught a glimpse of two of them walking side by side.

The red lip of the sun came up at that very moment, and before Joram's eyes, both beasts were changed instantly into the forms of men, who went on walking eastward toward the rising sun.

The men walked several miles into the rough hill country that lay in that direction, until they came to the tallest hill Joram had yet seen. He saw a thin trail of wood smoke rising from the top of the hill, and watched the two men head directly toward that place. He followed until he saw them disappear inside a house near the summit.

Joram hid himself in a deep thicket to watch, and by and by several more people came out of the woods and entered the house as well. He waited until no more came, and to make certain no one left the house.

The hilltop was flattened, and cleared of trees all around the house. Part of it was fenced, although Joram saw no animals or crops nearby. It was a bad place for farming, to be sure, for the dirt was too rocky and thin to grow much. Indeed there was a large flat stone thrust up from the ground at the very top of the hill, and smaller outcrops in several other places. It puzzled him why anyone would choose to live in such a poor place, but he decided perhaps the people were hunters or trappers who traded for food. He marked well where the hill and the cabin lay, and then returned to his own home.

Joram went secretly to the hilltop several times to spy on the people who lived there and to find out what he could about who they were. He began to notice that the cabin was usually empty, except near the times when the moon was full, and that the beast-men never stirred from their sleep till late afternoon.

So it was that he crept to the edge of the hilltop one morning in October, and hid himself inside the goat barn. It was to be the full moon that night, and he wished to see what happened when these men became beasts.

But that night was not to be like other nights. When the moon rose, he watched through a crack in the barn wall while ten people gathered silently around the flat stone at the top of the hill. They looked like ordinary people to Joram, and they did nothing but stand there in a circle.

Before long, a young man was led out of the house by an older man, and these two walked to the flat stone. It was a cold night, but the young man removed his shirt and lay down on his back on the stone.

Joram feared he was about to see the young man's death, but instead the older man held up a bowl high above his head, and then painted some of whatever it contained on the young man's chest with his thumb. Then he offered him a drink from a flask he held in his pocket, and the liquid it contained was so dark and thick that it might well have been blood.

When all this was done, the men and women in the circle looked up at the moon and howled, and before Joram's eyes they changed into the hideous beasts that had haunted his farm all that summer and fall.

The man with the bowl laughed, and then he changed form as well. Then all of them ran away into the woods.

Joram stood frozen with horror and fear in the goat barn, not daring to leave the place because of the beasts in the woods.

Now Joram had seen enough. He was a righteous man, and he fell to his knees and begged God to save him from the beasts, and to destroy this horrible place where so much evil had been done.

Then Joram fell senseless to the floor, and he was given a dream of what he must do. When he woke, he found a spring of cold water nearby. Then Joram blessed that water and gathered some of it in his canteen before sprinkling it everywhere on the hilltop, and especially on the flat rock. The young man still lay fast asleep on the stone, and the water did not wake him, not even when the paint was washed away from his bare chest. Then Joram prayed for that place to be clean again, and before his eyes the flat stone turned from gray to brown.

Then he set fire to the cabin and the barn, and fled from that place for the last time.

No beast ever came to trouble Joram or his family ever again, and no sight was ever seen of them in any of the lands nearby.

Joram never returned to the hilltop, but it may be that the blessing holds true on that place, such that no evil thing dare go near it.

All these things were told me by my grandfather, many years ago, and he always spoke the truth.

* * * * * * *

That's where the story ended.

I wasn't sure what to say. It feels really weird to think you're living in a fairy tale, you know.

I wondered how much of the story was true and how much was made up. Stories sometimes get garbled and twisted when people tell them over and over again. People forget things, or don't remember right, or add stuff that didn't really happen just because it sounds better. This one sounded true, but then they always do unless you know better.

I thought about the fire damage on the bottom corner of the journal and wondered if it came from when Joram burned down the cabin on top of Wolf Mountain. I was sure that's where the story was talking about, even though it didn't give the name. It had to be, since that's where I found the spring. I wondered if he was the one who carved the letters in the stone, or if somebody else had found that place and figured out what it could do in all the years since then.

"Look in the footnote section in the back of the book and see if it says where they found that story," Eileen told me. I leafed through the book until I came to that part.

"It says it was based on a story the author heard from a lady named Miss Edith Ross in Red Lick, Texas, in 1939," I said, once I found the right place.

"That's an awful long time ago," Eileen sighed, "I'm sure Miss Ross has probably passed away by now."

"She'd have to be at least eighty-something by now, even if she was a teenager when she told that story, and I bet she was older than that," I agreed, doing the math real quick in my head.

"When was that book published, Zach?" Eileen asked me. I looked at the copyright page and found it.

"Looks like 1944," I told her.

"Then the editor is probably gone by now too. I want to check one more thing, though," she said.

She started flipping through *Legends of the Red River Valley* again, and finally found what she was looking for.

"Here it is. A story by Edith Ross in Red Lick, Texas. It's got to be the same one," she said.

I got up and stood behind her so I could read over her shoulder. I always hate it when people do that to me, but Eileen didn't seem to notice.

The story was a little different than the version in *Tales of the Piney Woods,* but not very much. It left out the part about Joram blessing the spring, and it said he hid in a tool shed instead of a goat barn. In this version the beasts were called werewolves, and Joram shot the one he saw at Red Lick before he ran away. There were other changes like that. Nothing really major, but enough to make me wonder what really happened. The gist of the story was the same, but the changes bothered me.

"It looks like we may have to be content not to know for sure," Eileen finally said.

"I'm still glad I heard the story," I said. Reading about Joram and the way he fought the wolves and won. . . it really touched me down deep, exactly where I needed it right then. It made me feel like I was part of something that went back a long time, and that what I was doing really mattered. Joram was just an ordinary dirt farmer, from a place not very far down the road from me. If he could stand up and strike a blow against evil, then surely I could do it. Couldn't I?

Eileen smiled.

"I'm glad we heard it too, bubba. If there were more people like Joram Ross then the world would be a better place," she said.

"I really want to be like that," I told her.

"Maybe you will someday, Zach. Maybe you will," she said.

I think that's when I truly decided to put away all my second thoughts about what I was doing, and not to look back anymore. Up till then I still wasn't totally sure I wanted any part of being the Curse-Breaker. After Joram, I did.

"Do you think Miss Ross could still be alive?" I asked. I couldn't help thinking how much I'd love to talk to her, to see if she had anything to add and to let her know how much that story meant to me.

"It's always possible. But even if she is, she might be hard to find," Eileen said.

Just about that time, Justin and Cameron walked into the kitchen and I got distracted.

"Where have y'all been?" I asked.

"Down by the lake, talking about things," Justin said, "you were asleep for quite a while, you know."

"Oh, okay," I said. Or something like that. Eileen always says to tell the truth and shame the devil, so I'll go ahead and admit it. I was just a tiny little bit jealous. Justin wasn't supposed to be spending all afternoon talking to somebody else down by the lake. That was something me and him always did. I was too surprised and embarrassed to tell him I felt that way, but it's a fact.

I'm sure he noticed something was up, but he had the grace not to mention it right then.

"We found some good stuff today," Eileen said brightly. It ended what could have turned into an awkward silence, and I was glad for that.

"Yeah? Tell us about it," Justin said.

So Eileen told them about it while I sat in my chair and pretended to listen. I nodded every now and then and made a comment when it seemed called for, but I really wasn't thinking about Joram Ross anymore.

I was thinking more about Cameron and what exactly was going to happen with him. There hadn't been time to think much about it up till then, but that time he spent at the lake with Justin today had me thinking a lot.

Was he going to stay with us for a few days? A week or two? Months? I realized I had no idea. To be fair, I'm not sure he did either, but I decided me and him needed to have a serious talk about things as soon as possible.

I wondered what it was he and Justin had been talking about down by the lake, and I had another twinge of jealousy. I choked it down and didn't let it show on my face, but it was real, and I didn't like feeling it.

I decided not to think about that either.

The others were still talking about Joram Ross and wondering out loud if it would be worth going back out to Wolf Mountain to look for anything that might be left up on the summit to see if we could verify the story.

"The next closest stone is in Ruston, so why don't you all drive over there tomorrow and get rid of it, and I'll stay here this time and see what I can find," Eileen said.

"You're not coming?" Justin asked, turning to look at her in surprise.

"No, babe. I think I'll sit this one out," she said.

"Any special reason?" he asked.

"Yeah. I want to do some more research about all this. I may drive down to Shreveport tomorrow and see what I can find there," she said.

"Well, if that's what you want to do, babe," he finally said, sounding doubtful.

"Yeah, I think I will. You never can tell when it might be important," she said.

So that's what we ended up doing. In the morning we picked up our silly little silver dragon daggers and headed for Ruston. It was maybe a three or four hour drive, and there wasn't much to look at besides pine trees. On the other hand, I think everybody in Louisiana drives at least fifteen miles over the speed limit, so that added a little excitement to the trip. Driving on the interstate felt kinda like riding in a racecar. I peeked at the speedometer and saw that Justin was going at least 80 mph, and people were still flying by us like we were standing still. It was pretty awesome. If you don't believe me, just go drive that stretch of I-20 between Shreveport and Ruston and see what you think.

Anyway we got there without any problems, and then we had to find the place. This rock wasn't out in the country like the other one was, and that made it harder.

I kinda like Ruston, as towns go. It's hilly and has lots of wide streets and pecan trees. Maybe college towns are always like that. They have to be nice looking so students will want to come there.

Anyway, we hit a snag when we pulled into a parking lot and tried to make sense of the map in the journal. Maybe it's because the map was so old and Ruston has grown so much since then, but we could *not* find the place.

I knew where it was supposed to be. It ought to have been not far off the main highway that led north out of town. The only problem was, it wasn't there.

What *was* there, the best I could tell, was the parking lot of the Regions Bank.

"Well, this is a pretty pickle," Justin said dryly.

"It's got to be here. This is where the map shows," I insisted.

"I don't doubt it, Zach. But you see there's nothing here," he pointed out.

"Yeah, I can see that," I agreed unhappily.

"Maybe they paved over it when they built the parking lot. This place doesn't look that old," Cameron suggested.

"Maybe, but how can we get to it if it's under all this concrete?" I asked. Cameron shrugged; he had no ideas about that one.

"Look at the map again and make sure this is the right place," Justin said.

I got out of the truck and went to the edge of the highway, then paced due west the exact number of paces the map said I ought to take. I ended up right in the middle of the parking lot, just like I thought.

"Well, unless we start bustin' up the concrete with a jackhammer, there's no way to reach this one," Justin said.

"We can't just leave it at that," I insisted.

"We may have to, Zach. Surely you don't think anybody could use this one anyway, do you? Not when it's buried under six inches of concrete and rebar," Justin pointed out.

"No, but-" I started.

"But what?" he wanted to know.

I had no answer to give him.

"There's got to be something we're not thinking of. I don't know what it is, but there's got to be something," I insisted doggedly.

"I'm open to suggestions," he said.

I thought furiously.

"Are you sure you're starting from the right place? The road might be in a different spot than it was in 1863, you know," Cameron said.

"That's true, but the map has been updated since then," I reminded him, "We might be off a little bit, but it couldn't be much. We could just pace back east or a little farther west and see what we find. The stone would still be on the same line."

"Well, try that then. We've got nothing to lose," Justin said.

"Sure, why not?" Cameron agreed.

We started pacing west across the parking lot, and I'm sure we must have looked ridiculous out there. We walked all the way until we crossed Honeysuckle Lane and then even for a little bit into the woods on the other side. We didn't dare go too far in that direction though, because we'd start getting into people's backyards.

"I don't think it could be any farther in this direction," I finally said.

"Are you sure? It's better to keep going till there's no doubt about it," Justin said. I looked ahead of us and then back the way we'd come.

"No, it couldn't be ahead," I said.

"All right, then. Back we go!" Justin said cheerfully. We walked back to the edge of the bank parking lot, and then paced due east. There was a grassy area across the highway from the bank, and it was obvious just from looking at it that there was no stone anywhere over there. The only feature on that whole block was a clump of bushy trees down at one end.

"Come on, let's walk it anyway," I said, without much hope.

We crossed the road and paced it out, until we came to the next major street and had to stop. There was nothing on the other side except another parking lot and some buildings.

There didn't seem to be much point in going any farther.

"Come on, this is not getting us anywhere," I said.

There was a cross street connecting the two sides of the highway, and instead of walking back through the grass we took the sidewalk instead.

"If there did used to be a stone here, then it's gone now," Justin said, "They've either paved over it, or blown it up, or busted it to pieces with a bulldozer."

"We still didn't check those bushes," I said, still not wanting to give up. Justin and Cameron didn't say anything, so I headed for the trees. They were only a half a block away.

When I got there, I walked in among them and found busted pieces of concrete with rebar sticking out, and some humps of dirt and pieces of trash. It looked like a place where construction crews had piled leftovers from a building project and then green stuff had grown up all around it. Maybe that's why they didn't try to mow that spot like they did the rest of the block.

"Look!" Cameron cried out, and I turned to see him digging under a big slab of concrete. I went to see what he was doing, and Justin wasn't far behind me.

When I got there, I saw him pulling pieces of rubble off the top of a familiar-looking charcoal-gray stone. It was almost totally buried under dirt and shattered concrete, and the only part you could see was the very tip. It was a thousand wonders Cameron had ever spotted it.

I don't think that stone in Ruston had been used in a long time, and I doubt it was even possible to use it the way it was buried and half smashed like that. I wasn't taking any chances, though.

We spent most of the afternoon uncovering it, till we had more than half the surface clear. That big concrete slab like to have killed us when we pushed it off, and even all three of us together just barely had the strength to move it.

As soon as we had the stone cleaned off, we prayed over it and sprinkled the surface with water from the spring.

The same thing happened as it had at Greggton the day before, and as soon as we were sure it was clean, we got out of there.

We did the same thing the next day to the stone in Poplar Bluff, Missouri. That one was no trouble at all except for being so far off the road. We had to walk almost three miles through the woods to reach it, but that was about all. We nailed it quickly and left.

"Just two left," I crowed when it was done.

"Yeah, but those two are the ones that will be the hardest," Justin reminded me.

That sobered me a little, because I knew he was right. Of the two that were left, one of the stones was at the deer camp me and Cameron had escaped from, and the other one was in the middle of my mom and dad's apple orchard, within sight of their back door. Both of them would have wolves close by, no matter what time we went. Nothing was likely to be easy from here on out.

Chapter Ten

We came into Lebanon late one evening, and I was nervous. No, scratch that. I was terrified, more like it. I just knew we'd run into Mama or Daddy or at the very least somebody I knew, and that could wreck everything.

It wasn't just me who had a problem, either. My parents would surely recognize Justin, too, and maybe even Cameron. I didn't know how well they and Nana Maralyn kept up with the other wolves and their families. Even Eileen wasn't a sure thing, since they knew where I lived and they might have seen a picture of her or something. Maybe I was just being paranoid, but sometimes it's hard not to be, in situations like that.

We went to a little motel close to the interstate and parked away from the street so nobody would see Justin's Texas license plate and get suspicious. I know, I know, it was probably a bit much, but you can never be too careful.

It was a drizzly, cloudy kind of day, and it had turned a lot colder overnight. Sometimes summer ends that way, sudden as the snapping of a rotten branch in the wind. Just yesterday it had still been hot and sultry as ever, but no more.

Eileen went to the car rental place and got a car which was about as ordinary-looking as she could find. It was a white Mercury Sable, with dark-tinted windows that might possibly keep people from seeing who was inside.

It was strange being back in Tennessee. I kept seeing things I remembered, but somehow it was all different, too. I'm not sure why. Maybe it's because I was older now and didn't see things the same way I used to. Or maybe it's because anytime you're away from a place for a long time, it slowly accumulates little changes which you wouldn't have noticed if you'd been there the whole time, but the whole mass of them seems like a lot. I felt a strange combination of homesickness and fear which left a bad taste in my mouth.

I didn't say anything about it, though. I just kept telling myself we were there to do a job, and the sooner it got done the sooner we could leave.

I remembered the way, and we drove the Mercury out past my mom and dad's house. You couldn't see the actual house from the road, just the lane that led up the hill to it. Eileen didn't slow down since there was nothing to see and no reason to look suspicious.

"I think I know a way to get up close to the house without getting caught," I said, after we were past the lane.

"How's that?" Eileen asked, without taking her eyes off the road.

"If you turn left on the next dirt road, it goes back through the woods a couple of miles to an old rock quarry. Me and Jonathan used to go target practice back there. If we park the car then we can walk through the woods and come up on the back side of the apple orchard," I said. I'd done it lots of times, and even if the trail was gone, I was sure I could find my way.

"How far is it from the quarry to the orchard?" Justin asked.

"I don't know for sure. Maybe half a mile or so," I guessed.

"Well I can't think of anything better, so we'll try that first," Justin decided.

Eileen turned onto the dirt road and followed it into the woods, and before long we came out in the open again. The old quarry was more wide than it was deep, and you could drive down in there and park on the bottom of it. There was a gentle slope, and it was ringed on three sides by cliff walls that had been formed when they dug the rock out of the ground.

Down at one end it had filled up with rain water and formed a wide pool that reflected the sky and the rocks above it, because they rose directly out of the water on that side. Nobody knew how deep the pool was since you couldn't see the bottom of it and nobody had ever been able to dive or swim that far. You could jump off the top of the cliff into the water and not worry about hitting anything, but if you went down very deep then the water got so biting cold you couldn't stand it, so it was no fun to try.

There were some massive boulders and chunks of rock scattered around the area, and it was littered with coke cans that were punched with bullet holes or torn open by shotgun shells. There were also some broken glass bottles and a few plastic ones. Plastic isn't as satisfying to shoot at as cans or glass bottles, though, so there weren't as many of those.

People had spray painted their names on the rocks in various places, and sometimes other things. It was a place I always used to love when I was little, and seeing it again after all this time gave me that same feeling I had when we first got to Lebanon or when we passed my parents' driveway, only more so if you know what I mean.

Nobody was there, which wasn't too surprising since it was ten o'clock on a Friday morning. Most people were either at school or at work.

I probably should have been at school myself, for that matter, but I figured this was one of those times when it could wait. I was a good student, so they most likely wouldn't say too much about me missing a week. At least I hoped not.

We got out of the car and I scuffed my feet on the ground and walked up to one of the bigger boulders. There was a flake knocked off and a deep gouge in it close to the right hand side, and I put my finger up to it. There were a hundred others just like it, but I was the one who put that particular hole in that particular boulder, shooting at a Mountain Dew can with Jonathan's .22 one Saturday afternoon in November, not long before I ran away. Like I've said before, it's funny what you remember sometimes.

The others just watched me to see what I was doing, and I was suddenly embarrassed. This was no time for *déjà vu* or nostalgia or whatever the heck it was that I was feeling.

"Yeah, the house is this way," I said, and headed back uphill till I came to the edge of the woods on the far side of the dirt road. I had to nose around a little bit until I found the trail, but I remembered well enough. It was overgrown and weedier than I recalled, but it was still usable.

We slipped along the trail quietly, with me leading. I was pretty sure nobody would be out there right now. Mama and Daddy and Nana Maralyn went hunting back in those woods when there was a full moon, but I couldn't remember them ever going back there any other time.

Daddy would most likely be at work, and Lola would be at school. Nana Maralyn was almost always home, but she usually liked to watch the morning talk shows before lunch. Mama could be anywhere, but I doubted she'd be in the orchard. The apples would be long gone by now, and that's the only reason I could ever remember her going out there for, to pick them for pies and jelly and such.

We walked till we came to the barbed wire fence that divided the apple orchard from the woods. It was heavily overgrown with honeysuckle vines and wild mimosa trees, but that was okay. The trail led to a place where the wires had been cut, and you could push aside the vines and walk through if you liked. Nothing had changed about that part when we came to it. It was just the same as it always was.

I stopped before barging through, just to peer through the leaves and make double sure there was nobody in the orchard.

There didn't seem to be. I could catch a glimpse of the house fairly far off through the apple trees, but I didn't see a soul.

I did see the stone, though. It looked just the same as always, too, and my first thought was to be creeped out because this was the very stone where Nana Maralyn had tried to curse *me*.

No matter, I told myself. It wouldn't get used again!

"Come on, there's nobody here," I said out loud, and pushed aside the honeysuckle vines so I could step out into the open. Justin and Eileen and Cameron followed me, and ten seconds later we were standing by the stone.

I took out my last bottle of water from the sweet spring, and as usual sprinkled about half of it over the surface of the stone. Then we prayed over it, and we watched the dark gray start to change color like it always did. I was just starting to relax and tell myself this was another easy success story when I heard a sharp *thwack* right beside me, and felt a stinging chip of apple bark hit the side of my face.

Nobody who's familiar with guns can ever mistake the sound of a bullet hitting a tree. Especially not when it's that close to hitting *you*.

"Run!" I yelled, and wasted no time taking my own advice. I didn't know who was shooting at us and at that point I couldn't have cared less. All I wanted was to get away from them.

I was the first one into the trees, and Justin and Eileen were right behind me. Cameron was the last one, but we all made it okay.

Whoever it was hadn't given up yet, though, because every now and then we still heard the sound of bullets flying through the woods. Their aim wasn't too good since they couldn't actually see us very well, but they got a lot closer than I would have liked. Justin still had the pistol with the silver bullets in it, and after a few minutes he took the time to stop and fire a shot back at whoever was shooting at us.

That must have given them something to think about, because the shooting stopped after that. We ran down the trail till we were out of breath and had no choice but to slow down, but we didn't stop.

"That was another close one," I said, and tried to laugh. My hands were shaking and my knees felt watery and I don't think I've ever been so scared in my entire life, but I didn't want to admit it. If you've never been shot at, it's not something you want to try for kicks, believe me.

"It's not over yet. Shut up and get back to the car!" Justin hissed. I couldn't remember him ever being so rough before, but I can't say I blame him. Like I said, getting shot at has a way of upsetting people.

We partly ran, partly walked the rest of the way back to the quarry, and there were no more shots fired. We got to the car all in one piece, and in fact Eileen was already in the driver's seat and had the motor started when another bullet blew out one of the back windows. Me and Justin scrambled inside not a second later, and Cameron had his door open to jump in the back seat when the next bullet caught him square in the back.

He fell the rest of the way into the rear seat, and Eileen slammed the car into drive and hit the gas without even waiting for his door to get shut. She spun around in the gravel and threw up massive clouds of dirt, and she managed to bust out a tail light against one of the smaller boulders on her way out of the quarry. I hadn't known she could drive like that.

I heard several more bullets, but no more of them scored. Which is a good thing, I guess. It would be hard enough to explain a shattered window and a busted tail light to the car-rental folks, let alone bullet holes.

Once we got a little way down the road and out of range of any more shots, Eileen slowed down and drove more like a normal person instead of a crazy woman.

Cameron was groaning in the back seat and his door was still swinging back and forth. His feet were hanging out part way.

"Stop! We've got to see about Cameron," I yelled. We were almost to the highway by then, and Eileen stopped just long enough for me to pull Cameron farther inside and shut his door. That's when I noticed how much blood there was.

I don't do blood very well. I can handle it when I have to, but lots and lots of it just doesn't make my stomach feel too good. There was lots and lots of it on Cameron and underneath him. So much of it had soaked into the car seat that you could have wrung it out with two hands. And when I lifted him up, I saw blood welling up from his chest a lot faster than you would have thought possible.

I may not be a doctor, but I knew that was bad. Really bad, in fact. I also remembered my way around Lebanon well enough to know it would take at least twenty minutes to make it to the nearest hospital, and judging from the way he was bleeding, Cameron probably didn't have that long. He might bleed to death before we could even get him there.

For a second I was too frozen to think, and then I remembered something. I pulled out the last bit of water from the Sweet Spring and poured some of it on Cameron's chest and on his back where the bullet had gone in, and then I opened his mouth and dribbled a little bit inside, praying it wasn't too late. He was still awake enough to try to spit and sputter, but I held his mouth shut and he finally swallowed it.

The first thing I noticed was that he stopped bleeding so much, and gradually it slowed down to a trickle and stopped. He was still soaked in it, and so was I by that time, but no more was flowing.

Not long after that, he opened his eyes and looked up at me.

"Here, drink this," I told him, and held the bottle up to his mouth. He drank the rest of it, and in another minute or two he groaned.

"What happened?" he asked.

"You got shot in the back," I told him.

"Hurts bad," he said.

I was sure of *that,* I thought to myself, but I was glad to see him awake and talking again.

By the time we made it downtown, Cameron was sitting up in the back seat. He lifted up his t-shirt and looked at his chest, and underneath all the blood and mess there was nothing but smooth skin. I was too awed and shell-shocked to comment.

"I see it, but I can hardly believe it," Justin said.

"How do you feel, Cameron?" Eileen asked. He thought about it for a while.

"It still hurts a little, but not as much as it did before. And I feel dizzy and kinda sick, but I think I'll be okay," he said.

"Yeah, I think you will," Justin said.

Eileen slowed down and turned off her flashers, and instead of going to the hospital we drove back to the motel.

Justin went inside and got a navy blue blanket off one of the beds and brought it outside to wrap Cameron in, so nobody would see the blood all over him. He made a horrible sight, if you didn't know better. Then he handed me a towel. There was blood all over my shirt, so I took that off and threw it in the floorboard and put the towel around my shoulders instead. There was quite a bit of blood on my jeans too, but they were black denim Wranglers and you couldn't really see it unless you looked close or touched it.

We went inside, me shirtless and shivering in the cool breeze, and Cameron stripped off his bloody clothes and took a shower. When he got out and put on some fresh things he seemed as good as new. He still felt weak and sickly, but he had no marks on him.

Maybe it took a while for the water to work on something that major. I couldn't really blame him for feeling cruddy after an experience like that. As soon as he was done cleaning up, I stripped off my bloody clothes and took a shower too.

When I came out of the bathroom, Cameron was lying down on the bed fast asleep, and then the rest of us talked.

"It's a miracle. Nothing less," Justin whispered, looking at the pile of bloody clothes by the bathroom door. He already heard about what happened to me when I fell down the rocks, of course, but maybe seeing it happen in person like that made a bigger impression on him.

"Yeah it is," I agreed, "but what do we do now? The wolves must know what we're up to at this point."

It's not that I didn't feel just as much wonder and awe as Justin did, and it's not that I wasn't grateful that Cameron was still alive after what happened. I was, both of those things. But if there's anything I ever learned from him and Eileen, it's to stay focused when I have to.

"He's right, babe. We're still in danger here, too, if they come looking for us," Eileen reminded him. Justin nodded and shook off his awe-struck mood.

"Yeah, y'all are right. The first thing we need to do is get out of Lebanon, but first we need to do something about the car while things are still open. We can't take it back to the rental place all banged up and full of blood like that. It would make them ask way too many questions, maybe even call the police," he said.

"What can we do?" I asked.

"There's got to be a junkyard somewhere around here. We'll yank out that back seat and replace it with another one. They'll never know the difference. Same with the window. We might have to fess up to breaking the tail light, but that's not such a big deal," he said. Then he turned to look at Eileen.

"Will you stay here with Cameron and keep an eye on him while we're gone, babe?" he asked her.

"Sure thing," she said, and kissed him. It turned into a long one, and I looked away.

"Aw, come on, can't y'all do that later?" I finally asked.

"Yeah, guess so," he said, smiling at her. I rolled my eyes and pretended not to notice.

"Okay, come on, Zach," he said, and then he got up and headed for the door.

I couldn't remember where a junkyard might be in Lebanon. That wasn't one of the things I ever particularly needed to know before. My dad wasn't the do-it-yourselfer type, so he never took me anywhere like that. We found one in the Yellow Pages, though, and we drove the truck out there and bought the window we needed and a back seat. It wasn't quite the same color as the other one, maybe because it had faded in the sun a little bit, and there was a dark thumb-sized stain on it that looked like it might have come from a leaky pen. We hoped they wouldn't notice or care about the ink stain, but even if they did it would still be better than the blood.

We carried the stuff back to the motel and switched out the back seat without too much trouble. It was just held in with clips and screws, so it wasn't that hard to yank the bloody one out and replace it with the other one. We tossed the bloody one in the bed of Justin's truck.

Now that it was sitting next to the original upholstery, you could definitely tell that the new back seat was faded more than the rest of the car.

"I don't think that'll work, Justin," I said doubtfully.

"Yeah it will, just wait and see," he said.

I found Cameron's bullet lodged in the arm rest by the door handle while we were changing out the seat. I pried it out with my fingers and slipped it in my pocket without saying anything to Justin. It left a little hole in the arm rest, but with any luck nobody would notice that or guess what caused it.

The window turned out to be impossible for us to fix by ourselves, so we had to take it to a body shop and have them replace it. Justin gave them an extra hundred dollars if they had it done the same day, and you know it's amazing how fast they worked after that. We were out of there in less than an hour.

Then we went to an auto parts store and bought two cans of spray-on upholstery paint, which we used on the back seat. By the time we were finished spraying, it looked almost exactly like the rest of the car.

"Good deal," Justin said in satisfaction.

"Will that last?" I asked.

"Yeah, for a long time. It's not perfect but it will do," he said.

There was a scraped groove and a dent in the body next to the smashed tail light, and there was no way for us to do anything about that. We went back to the motel and fetched Eileen, then she returned the car to the rental agency. They made her fill out an accident form and she said they didn't act very pleased, but they didn't notice the switched seat.

It was almost dark by the time we got done with all that running around, but none of us wanted to spend another night in Lebanon if we could possibly help it.

We woke up Cameron and made sure the bathroom was clean, then we checked out of the motel and left.

It was a long ride back home, and we only stopped one time during the whole trip, to dump the bloody clothes and the car seat in the back of the truck. As soon as we got through Nashville, Justin started looking for a place to get rid of them, but we didn't find anything for a long time. He finally pulled off the interstate onto a country road that didn't look like it was used much, and we threw the stuff off a bridge into a muddy bayou.

Cameron kept his t-shirt with the bullet hole in it for a souvenir, but Justin made him scrub it clean in the water so nobody would see the blood.

The car seat didn't sink because of all the foam rubber in it, but it floated away out of sight downstream. That was okay. Even if somebody eventually found it and went to the trouble of pulling it out of the river, they'd never know where it came from. I don't like being a litterbug, but this was one of those times when it had to be done. We went to a car wash and Justin sprayed out the truck bed to make sure there was no more blood in it, and then he sprayed Cameron's t-shirt again until you couldn't tell what the stains on it might be.

Chapter Eleven

Not long after that we passed through Memphis and then crossed the Mississippi River into Arkansas. Cameron was quiet, looking out the window at the city lights across the water and listening to his mp3 player.

"Do you miss it?" I asked him, remembering he was from West Memphis himself.

"No, not so much. We always moved around a lot and it was no more home here than it was anywhere else," he said. He sounded kinda sad about it.

"Why did you move so much?" I asked.

"Well. . . Mama has this thing about going after cows and livestock. She won't stick to just deer and wild stuff. So she never could stay anywhere for long, because people notice that kind of thing. My dad used to keep her under control, but after he passed away then nobody could tell her anything," he said, and shrugged.

"I'm sorry," I said, "About your dad, I mean."

"Aw, it's okay, Zach. I can barely remember him, to tell the truth. It's always been just me and my mom, mostly," he said.

I wasn't sure what to say to him, and I wished I had Justin's way with words. He always knew the right thing to say.

"I saved something for you," I said, and pulled the bullet out of my pocket. He put out his hand and I laid the little piece of lead in his palm. He held it up to the light and looked at it for a few seconds.

"That's so cool," he finally said, and I could swear he even smiled a bit before he put it in his own pocket.

"You think it's cool what happened?" I asked, dumbfounded.

"Well. . . not the getting shot part, no, but I'm glad to be alive, that's for sure," he said. The conversation was starting to get uncomfortable again, so I changed the subject.

"So what are you listening to?" I asked him.

"Just some old stuff I like. Poison, Def Leppard, stuff like that. This is my favorite song of all time, though. Here, listen," he said. He handed me one of his ear buds and I put it in after making sure there was no wax on it.

He fiddled with the buttons on his mp3 player and changed it to a song I never heard before. It wasn't the kind of music I usually liked, but I listened to the lyrics since that's what people mostly want you to do anyway when they get you to listen to a song.

It talked about having good dreams and still being hated for it anyway and how nobody understood what that felt like, and things like that. It wasn't a very cheerful song at all, to tell the truth, but when I thought about it I guessed it was probably the way Cameron really felt sometimes. I couldn't blame him; I knew what that felt like myself, a little bit.

"It's called *Behind Blue Eyes*," he commented, watching me.

Sometimes you find a song that just seems like it was written for nobody else, and it's always eerie when that happens. This song fit Cameron that way. I wanted to tell him I understood where he was coming from and why he liked it so much, but for some reason I didn't do it.

I hate feeling tongue-tied like that.

"It's really cool," I finally said.

We didn't say anything else for a while, so Cameron took his other ear bud and went back to his music. As for me, I just looked out the window at the moonlight on the cotton fields and let my mind drift away. I had a lot to think about.

I thought about the future and all the things we might do with the spring once the wolf stones were all gone. There were so many hurts we could heal and so many sick people we could make better. The water didn't flow too fast, of course, and we'd definitely have to keep it a secret, but even so. . .

I smiled to myself. Justin always tells me I should spend my life to make the world a better place. I believe him when he says that, but I always used to wonder what there was I could do to make that happen. Crushing the wolf curse was one thing, true, but with any luck that would be over and done with soon. I didn't want my whole purpose in life to be finished when I was just fourteen years old. I wanted to find something I could spend the rest of my life doing, and it seemed like the Sweet Spring was a way for me to do that.

I had such big dreams.

We didn't get home till sometime after midnight, and by then we were all too tired to do anything but go to bed. We'd destroyed the last stone except for one, and even though that experience in Lebanon had turned out pretty rough, we still came through that one okay too. I had high hopes for the last one.

I still don't know who it was that shot Cameron and tried to nail the rest of us too. I don't really want to know. It had to have been either Mama or Daddy or Nana Maralyn, but knowing which one it was would be too hard. It would ruin whatever love I still have for them, and I found out that's something I'm not ready to give up yet. I keep thinking I'm ready to let go and forget about it; I even keep telling myself I've finally done it. But then it somehow seems to bubble up all over again at the strangest and most unwelcome times. Maybe it's something I'll always have to deal with, on some level. I know it's foolish of me, but there it is. I could no more change it than I could grow a third arm or a new foot.

Eileen always tells me that it's dishonest to willingly shut your eyes and choose to be ignorant when you don't have to be. And maybe she's right about that. I don't know. But I'm pretty sure she wasn't talking about something like which family member tried to kill you. That goes way beyond the pale of ordinary situations. And even if she *would* include something like that, I just can't do it yet. Sometimes when you're trying to face the truth, you have to open your eyes slowly so you're not blinded, the way you do when somebody first turns on the bedroom light early in the morning.

Justin always says that when you don't understand something or can't deal with it then you should pray about it. So that's what I did, and I felt better after that, and then I went to sleep.

In the morning we had a council of war.

"There's only one stone left, and the wolves know what we're doing now. If they didn't know before, you can be sure they do after what happened in Lebanon yesterday. This last one won't be easy," Justin said.

That was probably putting it mildly, I thought to myself.

"There's another problem besides that. We're out of water, too," Cameron pointed out. I noticed he was wearing something around his neck, and when I looked closer I saw that he'd strung his bullet on a necklace.

"We'd best go out there and get some more right now before we do anything else, then," Justin said.

"I agree. The wolves might find that place at any time, and once they do they'll destroy it," Eileen said.

"Come on then, let's go," I told them.

It was still early, and there was a chill in the air that made me shiver when I stepped out on the porch. It was cloudy and it smelled like rain, and a few of the leaves were beginning to change color on the sweet gum trees down by the lake.

We rode out to Wolf Mountain and instead of parking at the foot of it this time, Justin drove all the way to the top. The telephone company had a signal tower up there and I guess that's the main reason the road had been built and paved, but it suited us real well, too.

It was sorta pretty up there, once we came out on the flat top of the hill. You could see a long way in every direction. Off to the north and east the hills dropped off almost right away into a patchwork quilt of trees and farm land that stretched down to the Red River. I thought I could see the river itself, but there was no way to be sure. To the south and west the hills went on for a while and there wasn't much to see except trees. You couldn't see the city at all.

Justin always says you should never be in such a hurry that you can't enjoy beautiful things wherever you find them. I'm sure he's right about that, but we weren't here for sightseeing. We needed to get that water.

I was glad we wouldn't have to climb the hill today, since the spring was almost at the top.

Eileen was still curious about where Daniel Trewick's cabin might have been and that kind of stuff, so me and Cameron went to get the water and left her and Justin to do their archaeology or whatever you want to call it.

I knew the spring was somewhere to the northwest, but since I hadn't come in from this direction before I couldn't be sure exactly where.

"Come on, Cameron, help me look for a gully with lots of rocks," I said. We started out directly on the west side of the mountain where the road came in, and then worked our way north to make sure we wouldn't miss the place.

"You know, I never did thank you for saving my life yesterday," Cameron said after a while. He was playing with the bullet around his neck and looping the chain around his fingers.

"Yeah, don't mention it," I said.

"I have to mention it, Zach. I just want you to know I won't forget it," he said.

"Uh, you're welcome," I said awkwardly. The subject was embarrassing me.

"Hey, here's the gully," I said, partly to turn the conversation to a less uncomfortable topic.

It was indeed the gully, just as steep and rocky as I remembered it, and we soon decided there was no easy way to get down into it without a serious risk of somebody getting hurt.

"Come on, Cameron. It looks like there's no way down there unless we come in from the bottom," I said.

"You don't want to try the top first? It's a lot closer," he suggested. I thought about that, trying to remember if I'd seen any way down into the gully from the top. Try as I might, I couldn't remember.

"No, we don't have time for that," I finally said, "Let's just take the way we know."

Cameron nodded agreeably, and so that's what we did. It took us maybe twenty minutes to pick our way down to a place where the gully walls were low enough for us to get down into it without breaking our necks. Then we sloshed our way through the creek and over crumbling rocks back upstream.

We didn't get in any hurry, because I remembered what had happened last time when I was careless and nearly cracked my silly head.

Before long we slogged our way around the last bend to the rock wall where the spring should have been.

Except it wasn't anymore.

The rock wall was still there, blackened and cracked, but the area below it where the pool of water used to be was blown to smithereens. There was nothing there now but a pile of stony rubble.

I guess they must have used dynamite, maybe. I don't really know. But whatever they used, the Sweet Spring was no more.

We stood there and stared at it for several long seconds before either one of us said anything.

"I'm sorry, Zach," Cameron finally said.

"It's not your fault," I told him dully.

"Yeah it is, though. If you hadn't used the last bottle of water on me yesterday, then we'd still have some," he said.

That was true, of course, but what could anybody say to that?

"I'm not sorry for that, and you better not ever be sorry for it, either," I told him firmly.

There didn't seem to be anything left to say or do after that, and I couldn't have talked anyway past the big lump in my throat. I'm not even sure why it upset me so much, but I felt like a complete failure. Maybe it's because I had so much of myself wrapped up in destroying those stones and in my heart of hearts I'd truly come to think of myself as the Curse-Breaker by then. Whatever the reason, I felt like I'd let down everybody. . . Justin and Eileen, Cameron, Lola, all my little cousins, Joram Ross, and even God. That's a heavy burden, you know.

The explosion had destroyed enough of the gully walls that you could climb up to the top from there without too much danger, so I got down on all fours and started cautiously climbing up the rubble. After a minute Cameron followed me.

When we made it to the top I sat down on the edge of the blasted spring and looked back at what was left of it one more time.

I shouldn't have looked back.

Oh, I didn't get turned into a pillar of salt or anything, but I started to cry and that was almost as bad. I had to put my face down in my arms so Cameron wouldn't see.

He knew anyway, of course, but he had the grace not to say anything about it. He just sat there with me and let me cry it out till I was done. After a few minutes I heard him get up and move away, but I was too deep in misery to care what he was doing.

"Zach, look at this!" he cried, and I lifted my face to see what he wanted. He was back down the pile of rubble where the spring used to be, looking at something down close to the bottom of the rock wall. I couldn't tell what had him so excited and I was tempted not to care.

"What is it?" I yelled irritably.

I've noticed that it's hard to keep a cool head after you've been crying. You just can't talk to somebody at a time like that. It doesn't even matter how good the reason is or who it is that needs your attention. I think it must be a natural law. Cameron wasn't going to leave me alone, though.

"Come down here!" he yelled.

I got up, muttering to myself that I'd kill the boy if he didn't have a dadgummed good reason for harassing me.

It wasn't long till I made it down there where he stood, and then I stopped and crossed my arms over my chest. I was still surly and didn't try to hide it.

"What is it?" I said, scowling.

"Look here," he said, pointing to the rock wall. I leaned close to see what he was looking at.

The stone was wet. Nothing more than that, but when he touched his finger to the wetness and then brought it up to his tongue, I started to understand.

"Taste of it," he invited, smiling. Hardly daring to believe it, I reached out a finger and touched it to the cool stone, then lifted it to my lips and licked my fingertip.

The water was sweet, like honeysuckle nectar.

All my bad feelings vanished in an instant, and I looked at the wetness in fresh amazement. And while I watched, a single bright drop fell from the stone and lost itself in the rubble down below.

We watched eagerly for another one to fall, but it was a long, long time before it did. I caught that one in my bottle.

"Wait here and catch any more drops that fall; I have to go tell Justin and Eileen," I said, and Cameron agreed with a smile.

I clambered my way out of the rubble and headed directly for the top of the hill where the truck was parked. It was a lot faster to get there that way instead of retracing our steps back along the hillside.

When I came out of the trees I saw Justin and Eileen bent over looking at something on the ground near the phone tower. Eileen was facing my direction and saw me come out of the woods.

"Did you find it?" she called out. I ran across the clearing to where they were looking at whatever it was they were looking at.

"Yeah, we found it, but the wolves have been here and blown it up," I said breathlessly. They looked alarmed, and I hurriedly reassured them.

"It's okay, they didn't completely destroy it. It's still dripping a little bit, just not as much as before," I said. Justin frowned.

"I don't like the sound of that. A lot of times when you bust up the rock structure around a spring, it will just gradually dry up until there's nothing left. If there's anything still flowing at all, I suspect we'd better catch it while we can. It may not last long," he said.

I believed him. Justin knows all about geology, so when he says something about rocks you'd better take him seriously.

"Cameron is down there with a bottle to make sure we don't miss a single drop," I said. Justin nodded.

"That's good. Make sure he doesn't," he said.

"It sounds like we might be up here for a while, and I imagine we'll all be getting hungry before long, babe. What do you think about taking the truck downtown and getting us some food and things?" Eileen asked.

"Yeah, you're probably right," he said, "I just hate to leave y'all up here alone."

"We'll be okay for a while, I think. They've already been here and blown up the spring, so they probably won't be back. And then there are three of us, too, and I've got the pistol if we need it," she pointed out. Justin furrowed his brows and I could see that he wanted to argue about it, but then he seemed to change his mind.

"All right, babe. I won't be gone long," he promised. He held her for a long time before he left, and he even kissed me on the forehead. I guess all the stuff that happened in Lebanon was still fresh in his mind.

He got in the truck and started the engine, then rolled his window down.

"Be careful," he said one more time, and then he was gone. We watched him leave until the truck disappeared around the first bend in the road. Eileen sighed.

"I love that man. He has such a good heart," she said softly.

"Yeah, me too," I said. She put an arm around my shoulders and hugged me a little, then she got herself together.

"Come here, Zach. I found something interesting while you and Cameron were down at the spring," she said.

She took a few steps to the tower and squatted down so she could reach the ground. It was the highest point on the summit, and there wasn't much dirt there. She brushed away some sand and bits of grass to uncover the bedrock. It looked like ordinary brownish-red sandstone to me.

"Is there something you wanted to show me?" I asked.

"I think this might be the stone that Edith Ross talked about in her story, the one Joram broke the curse on," she said.

"Oh, yeah? What makes you think that?" I asked.

"Because it's at the very top of the hill, like the one in the story was. Of course it's been mostly buried and I guess partly crushed when they built the tower up here, but doesn't it remind you of the color the other stones turned after you blessed them?" she asked me. I took a closer look.

"Yeah, it does," I finally said.

"Come look over here, too," she said, getting to her feet. I did too, and she led me maybe a hundred feet to the west where there was somewhat of a depression in the ground and crouched down again.

There was a shovel lying on the ground, and somebody (I guess Justin) had dug a hole maybe a foot deep. That was about all it took to hit bedrock again, even there.

"See this?" Eileen asked me, pointing to the big divot of soil that lay on the ground beside the shovel.

"Yeah, what about it?" I asked.

"See this black layer? The soil is just a normal brown color above and below it, but here it's not," she explained. I saw what she was talking about. There was a thin black and gray layer which wasn't like the rest of the dirt.

"That's ashes and carbon from a fire that happened up here at some time," she told me. I was impressed.

"You mean this is where Daniel Trewick's cabin was?" I asked, getting interested at that point.

"Not necessarily. If the story is true then the fire happened in late October, and there would have been a lot of dead leaves and dry grass up here to burn at that time. Most of it would have washed away, but this little bowl would have caught some of it that flowed down from nearby. That's why we looked here. We'd have to dig all over the hilltop to find where the actual cabin might have been, if we ever found it at all," she said.

"So it doesn't really prove anything," I said.

"No, but it supports the story, gives it some evidence. Sometimes that's the best you can do. It's enough that I'm inclined to believe it really happened," she said.

"Did you find out anything in Shreveport the other day when you went?" I asked. I hadn't had time to ask her before now, and it seemed like a good time.

"I found Daniel Trewick's grave," she said.

"Really? What about it?" I asked.

"It just says he died in 1863 and that's about it. We already knew that much," she said.

"Oh. Well, I guess we should go help Cameron," I said. I was kinda disappointed, to tell the truth. I was hoping she had some big secret to tell me.

"I also talked to Edith Ross," she said, with a half smile.

"No way. How'd you find her?" I asked.

"It turned out not to be that hard. I just looked in the phone book," she said.

"So how did that go?" I asked.

"She still lives out there by herself in Red Lick, with about forty cats to keep her company. She's 97 years old now, I think she said. We had some sweet tea and sugar cookies and talked for about an hour or so," she told me.

"But what did she *say*?" I asked, impatiently. Eileen laughed.

"Patience, Zach. I'm getting there. She's a sweet old lady and still in her right mind, it seems. We talked about Joram and I told her a little bit about you and what we're doing with the spring. I didn't think it would do any harm. She believed everything, believe it or not. She also wanted you to come see her sometime," she said.

"She did?" I asked.

"Yeah she did. In fact she asked me twice to make sure and tell you that," Eileen said.

"I think maybe I will," I said.

"Good. I think you'd like her. But anyway, we better get down there and see how Cameron's doing. Justin's right about none of us needing to be alone for long. I just wanted to show you this stuff, and tell you about Miss Edith," she said.

We made our way through the woods to the head of the ravine where the spring was, and Cameron was still standing there with the bottle. He saw us as soon as we came to the top of the rubble heap and waved.

"I got three more drops!" he called up to us. It didn't sound like much, but I guess it was better than nothing.

We made our way down the rocky slope to keep Cameron company and take turns holding the bottle. After maybe an hour Justin got back with some cheeseburgers and fries, and we basically just waited.

We were there all afternoon, in fact. I don't know for sure how many drops of water we caught in the bottle. I lost count at about twenty-something. What I do know is that by the time it got dark we only had maybe two inches of water in the bottle we were using, and there hadn't been any more drips from the spring in at least an hour.

"I think that's the end of it," Justin finally said. The rock was starting to dry out where the drips had been coming from, and in my heart of hearts I knew he was right. The Sweet Spring was gone.

I looked at what we had, knowing there would never be any more, and for a while I thought again about all the wonderful things we could have done with that spring if it hadn't been destroyed. All the people we could have helped and who knew what else? None of that would ever happen now. It made me sad.

But Justin always says you can't ever expect God to do the same thing twice. That all of eternity isn't enough for Him to express Himself even once, and that you shouldn't be sorry for that, but instead look forward to whatever good thing He has in store next. If the story we read in the book was true, then the Sweet Spring was only meant for crushing this one particular evil, the answer to one man's prayer for help, and so maybe it was time for it to end now because its job was done. If I looked at it that way, then the wolves had only succeeded in fulfilling His plans anyway, in spite of what they thought they were doing.

I felt a little better about things when I thought about it that way. Justin doesn't always think I'm listening when he tells me stuff like that, but I try to remember what he tells me.

I said a silent prayer to thank God for this miracle, and then we climbed out of the gully for the last time.

I wondered what the wolves would do, now that they'd blown up the spring. Celebrate, probably. But would they leave me and Cameron alone now? They surely knew we'd destroyed the stone in Lebanon, and they might know about the others by now, if they were curious enough to go check them. Which they probably were. So they knew we'd found the spring and that we knew how to use it. The only thing they wouldn't know was whether we had any water left or not.

So what would they do? I tried to think what I might do if I was in their shoes. I think I'd probably spend most of my time trying to guard that one stone I had left, because I'd be sure that sooner or later either me or Cameron would show up and try to destroy it. There wouldn't be any need to look for us anymore. All they had to do was wait.

So if we went directly to Caddo Gap and attacked that last stone, then we'd be playing right into their hands, because that's probably exactly what they were expecting us to do. They'd be ready when we got there, and this time things might not turn out so well as they did at Lebanon.

On the other hand, if we didn't go attack the stone then that was also giving them exactly what they wanted. So what to do?

I honestly had no idea.

Chapter Twelve

We sat up late talking about it at the kitchen table that night.

"This is the last one, guys. When this is done, the wolves are finished. But they know that too, so this could be dangerous. We need to think and plan before we do anything hasty," Justin said.

He pulled out the topographical maps I'd found in Janelle Parker's Blazer and laid one of them out on the table.

"This is the area around the camp. Cameron, you lived with these people and stayed free for a long time. Do you know where the stone is?" he asked.

"Yeah, it's right in the center of the camp. That's the whole reason the camp is there," Cameron said.

That made sense, but it was going to make things difficult. We only had one shot at this, and we didn't need to mess it up.

"Are there always people at that camp?" I asked without much hope.

"Well, no. People use it in the fall and the winter for a hunting camp, and sometimes in the summer just for a campground. There's usually hardly anybody there between the end of deer season and when it starts to get warm weather again. You can never tell for sure, but I bet it would be completely empty in February or March, maybe," Cameron said.

"I see," I said.

"That's a long time to wait," Justin pointed out.

"Yeah, but right now is the worst possible time of year to go messing around with anything up there. It's full of people, and next month will be even worse, because everybody will be there for Logan's Ceremony," Cameron said.

"But what about when they hear about what happened in Lebanon? Won't they make sure to leave somebody there to guard the place all the time?" Eileen asked.

"They might, but they won't be able to stay there *all* the time. Most of them don't live close by, and they do have jobs and stuff," Cameron said.

"So do we, for that matter," Justin muttered, half under his breath.

"But what if they hire a guard or install an alarm system or put up an electric fence or something like that, so the place is watched all the time?" Eileen asked. Everybody was silent at that.

"That's a serious possibility, since they know this is the last stone. That's why I think we need to go ahead and get up there now, before they have a chance to do anything like that. I think the longer we wait, the harder it will be," Justin said.

"Yeah, you're probably right. I didn't think about that," Cameron admitted.

We all thought about that in glum silence.

"There's another reason not to wait very long, too. What about your mom, Cameron? Won't she be looking for you?" I asked.

"Yeah, she might, but probably not for the reasons you think. She'll know by now that I was there at Lebanon with you, and she'll never forgive me for that," he said.

I thought about that for a minute.

"What do you want to do, Cameron? I mean when all this is over?" I asked him quietly. I'd been meaning to ask the question for a while, but now seemed as good a time as any.

"I don't know. My mother will never let me come back home after she finds out I helped you, so. . . " he shrugged.

"So why did you do it, then?" I asked.

"I already told you why," he said, with a bark of laughter that didn't really sound like he thought it was very funny.

"Yeah you did, and I know they always treated you rotten, and maybe that was a good reason to leave for a while when you could. But you know your mom would have figured out it was me breaking the stones and not you, if you hadn't helped me. She wouldn't have had any problem with you after that," I pointed out.

"You don't understand," he said, looking down at the table.

"Explain it to me, then," I said. He took a deep breath and glanced at Justin.

"Justin knows why," he finally said. I turned and looked at Justin and raised my eyebrows.

"Let him be, Zach. He has a good reason," Justin said, putting a hand on Cameron's shoulder.

Justin doesn't ask for things without a cause, so I bit my tongue and didn't push Cameron any more. But I couldn't help wondering what all the secrecy was about. It annoyed me a little bit.

There was an uncomfortable pause.

"I have a plan for how we can do this thing," Cameron finally said. I was still irritated, but I tried not to show it.

"Spill it, then," I said.

"I think I should go to the camp and sneak in by myself, like I'm there to break the stone. I can carry a bottle of sugar water with me, and let the guards catch me with it. They won't do anything very bad to me I don't think; just lock me up again, maybe slap me around a little. But they'll think they caught the Curse-Breaker then, and maybe they won't be on their guard anymore. So if you're careful, you can sneak into the camp with the real water and get the job done before they know what happened," he said.

It seemed like the oldest trick in the book to me, but still, my mood softened when Cameron told me his plan. After what happened to him in Tennessee, I was amazed he could still talk like that. He knew very well what could happen, and there wouldn't be anybody around to save him this time if it did.

"That's the bravest thing I ever heard," I finally told him. It humbled me, to tell the truth. He shrugged and kinda smiled a little.

"Well, somebody's got to do it," he said, "and I stand a better chance than you do of not getting hurt. I know my way around the camp better, and everybody there has known me all my life. I don't think they'd be as likely to shoot at me as they would you."

"They nearly killed you last time," I reminded him.

"Yeah, but I didn't know them. That was *your* family, and you see who they shot at. So it really just proves my point, when you think about it," he said.

I don't know. . . maybe he had a point about that, much as I hated to admit it. But then again, that first bullet that hit the apple tree was aimed at *me*. I knew that just as sure as I knew anything, so Cameron might not be anywhere near as safe as he thought he was.

It was still hard for me to think about what happened in Lebanon, though.

"Won't they wonder where I am, if they only catch you?" I asked.

"Maybe, but that's probably the first thing they'll ask when they catch me, and if I can tell them a good enough story they might believe it," he said.

"Like what?" I asked.

"I don't know. Maybe I could tell them you got hurt really bad at Lebanon and I'm the only one left; they don't know the water would fix that," he suggested.

It sounded promising at first, but Justin shook his head.

"I don't like that idea. We don't know how much they saw, and if they figure out you're lying it would be worse than saying nothing at all," he pointed out.

"They couldn't have seen too much; they were too far away to know for sure if they hit anybody or not. I'll tell them we decided I should go ahead and come up here alone before they had time to put up a fence or hire a guard or any of those other things we talked about them doing. They might believe that because it makes sense," Cameron said.

"Won't they wonder how you got there?" I asked.

"Yeah, I'll tell them Justin brought me and dropped me off, and he'll be back to get me outside the gate in two hours. If I fight a little bit and make them work hard to get the story, I think they'll believe it. I know Logan and Heath will, because they're both stupid enough to believe anything. Laura's the only one I'm worried about. She's the one who calls the shots, and everybody else will go along with whatever she decides," Cameron said.

I believed him on that one. She'd definitely acted like she was the big cheese when I was locked up.

"You think you can convince her?" I asked.

"Yeah, I just have to act like I'm afraid of her. She likes it when people do that. She also thinks I'm a weakling who wouldn't dare stand up to her," he said calmly.

I could believe that, too. It sounded just like the way Laura would act; proud, pushy, and full of herself. And also cruel.

"You might get hurt," I warned him.

Cameron shrugged and fiddled with his bullet again.

"Nothing gets done without some risk," he admitted. Nobody said anything to that.

"Is it settled then?" he went on cheerfully, as if that was all there was to it.

"I don't remember agreeing to the plan yet," I pointed out.

"Do you have a better idea?" he asked, and of course I didn't have an answer.

"All right, you got me there. Let's do it," I sighed. It was the best plan any of us was likely to think of, and I knew it.

The next day it was raining when we left. I stood on the porch watching it come down, reluctant to make the dash for the truck. I hate going out in the rain. You get just wet enough to be damp and cold for hours. Eileen always likes to tell me I won't melt, so I knew better than to grumble about it. Nobody else seemed to care, so maybe I'm the only one who doesn't like to get soaked.

They all made it to the truck ahead of me, so I finally bit the bullet and ran out there myself.

Nobody said much on the way to Glenwood. I guess we all knew how serious it was and how dangerous this thing might be. Justin and Eileen were holding hands in the front seat and everybody seemed wrapped up in their own thoughts.

When we got to Glenwood Justin pulled out the topographical map and found a road that came as close to the deer camp as possible without actually leading to it, and then he drove us out there. It was still drizzly and muddy and cold, not at all the kind of day you want to be out walking in the woods, but none of us wanted to wait for it to stop.

Justin parked the truck and let us out. His job was to come with us as far as the top of the ridge and make sure we didn't need any help, and Eileen was supposed to man the getaway car so we'd be ready to bolt at a moment's notice if we had to.

We were in a steep valley where there wasn't much room for anything besides a little creek and a narrow, rocky road that snaked along beside it. The topographical map showed that the camp was right over the southern ridge from this valley, if we had our bearings right.

The three of us climbed the rocky wall of the valley, getting muddy and wet and trying our best not to dislodge any chunks of stone that might go crashing down into the valley and make a horrendous racket that would let the wolves in the camp know that something was up.

There was a curling wisp of wood smoke rising from just below us and to our right when we got to the top of the ridge, and we caught a glimpse of metal roofs. It was the camp.

"Good, we're right on target," I whispered. We picked our way west along the ridge top until we were even with the camp, and then we were able to look directly down into it.

"There's the stone," Cameron said, pointing to the far side of the camp. Sure enough, there it was. It was charcoal gray, just like all the others, and there was a circle of metal buildings around it. I glimpsed what looked like the building they had me and Cameron locked up in, but that was close to the nearer edge. The stone was all the way on the other side of the compound, past some other buildings and trees.

There didn't seem to be a lot of people moving around, but maybe that was because of the cold and the rain. I felt sure somebody was watching from inside those buildings.

"All right, wish me luck," Cameron whispered.

"Luck," I whispered back, and then he was gone. Me and Justin waited on the ridge top for him to show up down below. I didn't plan on going down there until about thirty minutes later. I wanted to give the wolves time to get careless.

"Zach, what would you think about Cameron coming to live with us for a while?" Justin asked me after a while.

"Um, I guess that would be all right. For how long?" I asked.

"Maybe for a long time. Maybe always," he said.

I didn't want to hear that. I was used to being the only one and I wasn't sure I wanted an instant brother, even if it was Cameron.

"I don't know what I think," I admitted honestly.

"Yeah, that's what I thought. Cameron thought so too, and that's why he hasn't said anything about it to you," Justin said.

"He said something about it to you?" I asked.

"Yeah, we talked about it that day down by the lake while you were asleep all afternoon. He said being with us was the first time in his life when he ever felt like he belonged somewhere, but he didn't want to horn in on you," Justin said. That made me feel kinda bad, honestly.

"He could have told me. I would have said it was okay for him to stay as long as it was okay with you and Eileen," I mumbled. Then I thought of something else.

"Is that why he's been helping us, because he wants me to like him and let him stay?" I asked, frowning.

"Don't be so quick to judge, Zach. And don't be so quick to put anybody's motives down to just one thing. I'm sure that's part of it, but I don't know that that's a bad thing. He's down there risking his life right now, not because of something he cares about, but because of something *you* care about, because you're his friend and he wants you to think well of him. That counts for something, doesn't it?" he said.

And you know, it *did* count for something. I guess I half-knew what Cameron was thinking all along, I just never quite faced it head-on.

"I'm sorry. I should have said something to him," I said.

"You probably should have," Justin agreed, "but it's not too late, you know. When all this is said and done, let him know you're glad to have him with us. I already told him so, and so did Eileen."

"You did?" I asked.

"Yup. But he won't stay unless you want him to," he said.

"But what would happen to him if I didn't?" I asked. Justin shrugged.

"He doesn't know. I guess he'd go somewhere, maybe back to his mom if she would let him, and if not that. . . who knows?" Justin said. I thought about that, and whatever doubts I might have had about letting Cameron live with us faded away. I knew what it was like to have nowhere to go.

"Did he ask you to talk to me about it?" I asked.

"No. I did that on my own," Justin said.

"I'll let him know," I promised.

"Good," Justin said, and ruffled my hair. We were quiet for a little while, but there was something else I wanted to say.

"Justin?" I asked.

"Yeah?" he said.

"I really love you. I hope you always know that," I said. He smiled.

"I know. I love you too, Zach," he said.

"Don't you ever get tired and wish you had more time for you and Eileen, though?" I asked.

"Well, you know, Gran and Paw didn't have to raise me and Jenna after Mama and Daddy died. And yet they did, for love's sake. Eileen didn't have to stay with me and take on a half-grown boy to raise just because I decided to, but she went ahead and did it anyway, for love. When you've been blessed, you don't hold the gift in your hands and try to keep it for yourself, Zach. If you do that, it turns to poison before long. You pass it on. Me and Eileen both agreed on that a long time ago, even before you came along. Her heart is even more beautiful than her face, and that's one of the reasons I love her so much," he said.

I remembered that Eileen had said something very much like that about Justin, back on Wolf Mountain, except not in so many words. When I hear things like that, it makes me love both of them all the more.

We sat close to each other on a flat-topped boulder and threw a blanket around our shoulders to keep warm. The drizzle showed no signs of letting up, and the wind was freezing.

"There's Cameron, I think," I whispered. I thought I recognized his blond hair and the camo jacket he'd been wearing, but at this distance I couldn't be completely sure. I watched him disappear under some trees before he popped back up in the circle where the stone was.

Then I heard the pop of a rifle, and Cameron hit the ground. Two guys ran out of one of the buildings close to the rock and bunched up around him. One of them got down to look at Cameron, and the other one actually jumped up and down and threw his arms up to the sky.

I wanted to spit on him for that.

"Easy, Zach," Justin said. I guess he felt the tension in my body or something, so I tried to relax.

It wasn't long before the two of them picked up Cameron and carried him across the compound to the building where both of us were locked up the first time. Then everything was quiet.

"Come on, let's head that way," Justin said in a little while.

"What are you talking about? I thought you were supposed to stay up here on the ridge and make sure we didn't need any help?" I asked.

"Yeah, well, it looks like you might need some," he said mildly.

We crept our way down the slick slope, trying not to lose our footing. As we got lower down we couldn't see the camp anymore for the trees, but that was okay. We knew where it was.

It was only a few minutes till we came within sight of the place, and then Justin put a hand on my shoulder to stop me.

"Come on, Zach. Let's circle around to the back of the camp instead of cutting straight through like Cameron did. They're less likely to see us that way. He wanted to get caught. We don't," he said.

That was good sense, so we made our way warily around to the other side of the camp. We could hear a little noise coming from the main building. It sounded like they were having a party over there. Somebody was playing music, and it must have been loud to carry that far. Other than that it was quiet except for the drizzle.

We were standing between two small buildings which I guess were cabins for people to stay in while they were at the camp. They were both empty as far as we could tell.

"Come on, let's do it," I said to Justin, in the lowest voice I could use. I took the bottle of spring water out of my pocket and loosened the lid so I wouldn't have to waste time later when I was out in the open. Then I took a deep breath and walked out from between the buildings.

I made it about halfway to the stone.

"Stop right there," I heard a voice behind me say. I turned my head and saw Laura, holding a pistol in her hand. I froze.

"I thought it was too easy, catching Cameron like that," she commented, "Looks like it's a good idea I stayed behind."

"Yeah, sounds like they're having a party over there without you," I said, and even managed a sickly smile.

"Oh, that's nothing to the party we'll be having when I get there with *you*," she said confidently.

"Look, you win, just be careful with that thing," I said, trying to look scared. It wasn't all that hard to do right then. I remembered what Cameron said about how Laura enjoyed it when people were afraid of her, and I hoped he was right. I had to keep her occupied as long as I could so she wouldn't notice Justin.

He was slowly and silently creeping up on her from behind. The music and the rain were loud enough that she couldn't hear his footfalls on the muddy ground, and I wanted to keep it that way.

"Did you really think you could get away with this?" she said, shaking her head like she couldn't believe I was that stupid.

Justin was almost behind her when he stepped on something that crackled under his foot, and Laura heard it. She whirled around and saw him, and I knew without being told that he was dead if I didn't do something.

I tackled her with my whole weight and knocked her to the ground. The pistol flew out of her hand, but not before she fired a round. It went wild and smashed into the wall of one of the cabins, but there was no way the people in the main building hadn't heard it.

The girl could fight like a tied coon, I have to give her that much. She was stronger than me and Justin both put together, and if the fight went on much longer she'd soon beat us down. Wolves are unbelievably strong, even on normal days. Justin grabbed the silver cross around my neck and broke the chain, then held it to her skin. She must have known what it was, because she froze.

"Now, Zach. Hurry!" he yelled at me. I didn't need to ask what he meant. I pulled myself loose even though Laura tried to hold on to me, and I ran staggering through the slick mud until I stood by the stone. I unscrewed the cap on the bottle.

"No, please!" the girl begged. I could almost have sworn she was crying, but it was hard to tell with the drizzle. Or maybe she was just trying to fool me until her buddies got there. Somebody had cut off the music and the lights over there when the pistol went off, so it was only a matter of seconds till they got here.

"Father, crush this place," I whispered, and shook the holy water on the stone. I heard Laura moan behind me and watched the color change from charcoal to sandy brown, and I knew the curse was broken on the last stone. I screwed the cap back onto the little bottle and stuck it back in my pocket.

We weren't done yet, though. I could see two men running out the door of the main building, and they were headed this way.

I ran to where gun was lying on the muddy ground and picked it up, then came and stood beside Justin. He got up, holding the sharp silver tightly against Laura's wrist, and she stood up beside him. She didn't try to get away, and when the men came up and saw the three of us standing close together, they stopped uncertainly. They had weapons, but so did we, and that made it a standoff.

"What happened, Laura?" one of them yelled. He was a big guy with hairy hands, and I guessed he must be the one they called Logan, the Werewolf Vet himself. Cameron had said he looked like Bigfoot in cowboy boots, and I could definitely see the resemblance. I still wanted to say a few things to the man, but I decided it wasn't such a good time for that. There are certain situations when you need to shut up and hold your tongue, no matter how good it might feel to tell somebody exactly what you think of him.

"The stone is broken. It's all over," Laura said bleakly, and they both turned to stare at it. I couldn't read their faces.

"Where's Cameron?" I yelled at them, and they actually flinched, like they were afraid of me or something.

"He's in the main building," the little guy said.

"Bring him out," I ordered them.

They hesitated.

"Go on and bring him out; it doesn't matter anymore now," Laura said.

The little guy went back to the main building, and not long after that he came back, leading Cameron. He looked pale and he walked slowly, like he was in pain.

"What's wrong with him?" I yelled.

"He got a bullet in the leg, and then he got roughed up a little bit. That's all," Logan said in a surly voice.

"I have a deal to make with y'all," I said, "I've got no more fight with any of you, now. Go do whatever you want to and I won't interfere. Just let Cameron come with me, and then stay out of our lives for good," I said. Cameron looked at me when he heard that, but he didn't say a word.

"Good riddance to both of you, as far as I'm concerned," Logan said.

"Hey, Logan, you can't just- " the other one started.

"Yeah, I can, Heath, so stuff it," Logan said. He grabbed Cameron by the scruff of the neck and gave him a hard shove toward us. He fell down in the mud, and Logan gave him a swift kick in the ribs for good measure.

"Stop that!" I cried.

"Oh, I'm done with him now," he said. Justin went and helped Cameron to his feet, and soon he was standing beside us. Laura pulled herself together and went to stand beside the two men. I didn't try to stop her.

"Just get out and never come back, both of you," she said. Then she turned on her heel and headed for the main building. After a second the two men followed her, leaving us standing there alone in the rain.

"We did it, bro. It's all over," I said.

Epilogue

Spring comes slowly, some years. I don't remember when I ever saw a colder and grayer winter than that one turned out to be. It's only been the last week or so that the grass has started to turn green and you can feel a little warmth in the breeze.

Cameron had a hard time with the cold, and that made it worse for all of us. He had a cracked rib and a lot of bruises from that last adventure, and he still limps on his left leg sometimes. He can't skate anymore, and I'm not sure if he will ever be whole again.

We sit together down on the dock sometimes with our feet hanging in the water and we talk about everything that happened, and how unlikely it all was. Sometimes we even laugh, but it's the kind of laughter that can live with sorrow at its heart. Maybe that's the best kind. We're very much alike, me and him. He may only be my third cousin, but he feels like my brother.

His mom sent him a box of clothes and things in the mail a few months ago, whatever stuff he still had left at her place. Other than that she's never tried to talk to him since we cracked the stones, and we both know she could have if she wanted to. I guess he was right when he said she'd never forgive him for helping us break the curse, any more than my family will ever forgive me. That's a bond we will always share.

I wonder if Mama and Daddy really hate me now as much as I was afraid they would. After what happened in the orchard last fall, I can't help thinking they must. That still stings once in a while.

But in spite of all that, I've learned the power of love to wash away tears, and even though the past may be sad, I wouldn't go back and change it now. Cameron feels the same.

We both still wonder about a lot of things, and sometimes when we talk we form some ideas about them. But I won't write them here. Not yet. They're just thoughts.

I've been to see Miss Edith a few times out in Red Lick. I mow the grass and rake her leaves and stuff like that, and then we sit on the porch and drink tea and talk about stuff. Last time I was there she told me not to be afraid of greatness and to always have the courage to grasp whatever task God may decide to lay in my hands. She reminds me of Nana Maralyn in a lot of ways, except nicer. More like the way I wish Nana Maralyn might have been.

I try not to think of my family too much. I'd still love to see my sister again someday, but whether I ever get to or not, I know she'll be safe from the wolf curse, at least. She may make her own mistakes and suffer her own sorrows in the world, but that will never be one of them. I hope she knows, somehow, that I was thinking of her. No matter what she might hear about me, I hope she knows what was in my heart. I hope all my little cousins know, too.

Cameron never talks about it much, but we all know he risked his life for love of Justin and Eileen and me. And yet, Justin and Eileen loved me and Cameron because other people had loved them first, and on back and back until it gets bewildering. It all links together, it all serves the purpose, and it all works to the good even when I can't possibly see how. I doubted that before, but I believe it now. At the heart of darkness, there's always a nugget of gold.

Did Justin's grandparents ever foresee that their kindness would someday be part cause of saving their great-grandchildren from sin? Did Joram Ross ever suspect that his prayer to God in 1863 would save a boy's life a hundred and fifty years later? I think not. I can trace some of the threads, but not all of them. And yet if it wasn't for Joram, and for Papa Wilder, and Gran Wilder, and Justin, and Eileen, and Miss Edith, and a hundred other people I've never met and will probably never know, then me and Cameron could never have done what we did, and the curse would still be alive today. It makes me wonder sometimes how much of what *I've* done is tied into the future like that, in ways I'll never know of.

It awes me sometimes when I think about it. Justin always says that if you pour light into the darkness for love of the light, then you'll never lack for a reward. I don't doubt for a moment that he's right about that, just like I never doubt that anything me and Cameron accomplished, we could never have done on our own.

I still wear my silver cross even though I don't really need it to defend myself anymore. I have a different use for it now. Whenever I reach up and hold it in my hand, I'm always reminded that nothing is too hard and no enemy is too terrible for God, and that we conquer through Love, or not at all.

End of Book Two

Enjoy this free sample of

More Golden Than Day
The Last Werewolf Hunter, Book Three

Guard your heart above all things,
For it is the wellspring of your life.
                    -Proverbs 4:23

Chapter One

The first time I ever saw Jolie was at the Four States Fair, the year I turned sixteen.

It didn't seem like one of those days when your whole life changes, and if you'd told me I was about to get dragged into the most dangerous and amazing experience of my entire life, I never would have believed it.

Or maybe I would have, come to think of it. I've been through a few tight spots in my life, and if I've learned anything, it's that you should always expect the unexpected.

I remember it was about nine o'clock or so, and me and Cameron were just getting ready to grab a bite to eat before we headed home for the night.

That's when I saw her, standing by the ticket booth and sipping on a can of Cherry Coke. I wouldn't usually have paid much attention, but she was so pretty I couldn't help giving her a second glance. She had long red hair with blonde streaks that glinted in the carnival lights, and she reminded me of a basketball player or maybe Lara Croft in *Tomb Raider*. Very athletic.

She must have noticed me looking, because she turned in my direction and smiled at me with a little wave. I smiled back and then walked over to say hi to her, since she caught me looking. Cam was too busy playing a game to notice.

"Hey, I'm Zach. Have we ever met before? You look so familiar for some reason," I told her when I got close enough. That was sort of a half-truth; she didn't really look familiar, but then again she kinda did. I couldn't decide for sure.

"No, I'm new around here, I'm afraid. I don't know much of anybody," she said.

"Really? Where are you from?" I asked.

"Natchitoches, Louisiana. Nowhere you ever heard of, I'm sure," she laughed.

"No, I guess not," I admitted.

"I didn't think so. Nobody ever has. My name's Jolie, by the way," she said. There was a pause, and I tried to think of something else to say.

"So what brings you up this way?" I finally asked.

"Oh, I just came to stay with my aunt for a few days. She lives up here all by herself, and she needs some help now and then," she said.

"Well, hey, me and my brother are fixing to go get somethin' to eat. You want to come with us?" I offered.

"Sure, why not?" she said.

She grabbed my arm as we left the ticket booth and I was kinda surprised at that. Most girls are not that flirty with somebody they just met, you know. I also noticed she was wearing what looked like a guy's high school ring on her left middle finger, and that made me wonder if she might have a boyfriend somewhere. If she did, then it was even stranger that she was being so touchy-feely.

I can't help noticing things like that, you know. Eileen always tells me I'll make a great scientist or a detective someday because I pay attention to little details that everybody else overlooks. Maybe so.

Cameron was done with his game by then, and when he saw us walking together he smiled.

"Hey, who's your friend?" he asked.

"Uh, this is Jolie. I asked her if she wanted to come eat with us," I said, and he turned to look at her.

"Hey, I'm Cameron. Don't believe anything Zach tells you about me," he told her.

"Oh, I'll try not to," she laughed.

She hooked one arm around mine and the other one around his, and the three of us walked together that way until we came to the food stands.

Me and Cam ordered some chili cheese fries, and Jolie got a basket of tater logs with nothing but salt on them, not even any ketchup. Maybe she didn't want to get anything drippy on her clothes; they looked kind of expensive, even though it was only jeans and a sweater.

The picnic tables were crowded that night and we had to squeeze close together to find a place for all three of us, but nobody minded that. We all laughed and joked and talked like we were old friends, and I remember thinking what a cool person she was.

Cam must have thought so too, because he snapped a picture of the three of us with his phone, like he always does when he's having a good time.

After a while Jolie put her arm around me and leaned over close like she was about to lay her head on my shoulder. I'm not sure what I would have done if she had, but as it turned out that's not what she had in mind.

"They're watching us," she whispered in my ear instead. She was so close I could feel her breath tickle the hair on my neck.

I have to confess I wasn't at my sharpest right then, and for a second I drew a total blank.

"Huh?" I said stupidly.

"Hush and don't look surprised. It's dangerous if they think this is anything but me having a good time at the fair. I don't know for sure if they can see us right this second, but I know they've been following me all day. Werewolves. Now kiss me and make it look good, like that's all we're thinking about," she said.

And that's exactly what she did.

I have to say, that was probably the last thing on God's green earth I was expecting. It felt more like a scene from *Mission: Impossible* than anything else. Go ahead and laugh if you want to, but I swear that's exactly what popped into my head, and I had to bite my tongue to keep from laughing.

Nevertheless, I managed to keep a cool head and kiss her back. Sort of.

She quickly slipped a piece of paper into my hand, and then she got up and looked at her watch like she just realized what time it was.

"Sorry, boys. Got somewhere I have to be in a little bit. See y'all later," she said, and then turned and walked away.

I watched till she was out of sight, still too astonished to comment, and then I looked down at the slip of paper she gave me. It said *Call me tomorrow!* and below that was a phone number. Cameron saw it too, and he just sat there looking at me with an annoying grin on his face.

"Oh, you got it bad, Zach," he finally said with a laugh.

"No I don't," I said. It was definitely one of the weirdest experiences of my life, and I didn't have a clue what to make of it yet, but I definitely didn't want Cameron thinking I was all swoony and calf-eyed over a girl I barely met. That was just too cheesy by half.

"Yeah, whatever. She's pretty awesome, though," he said.

"You think so?" I asked.

"Yeah, I do. You should give her a call tomorrow," he said.

"I don't know; maybe I will," I said.

"You'd be dumb if you didn't," he told me.

"Well, anyway, let's get out of here," I said, changing the subject.

It took forever to get out of the fairgrounds because of all the traffic, and I let Cameron drive. My mind was much too full to pay attention to the road right then. I've been told before that sometimes I think too much, but this was one time when I had a good reason for it.

Being kissed by beautiful and mysterious strangers who pop up out of nowhere isn't something that normally happens in my life, believe it or not. That by itself was enough to knock me back for a week, whether I admitted it to Cam or not.

But it was kinda scary, too, the more I got to thinking about it. Who *was* this girl, and how did she know about the wolves? And why did she think they were watching us on the midway tonight?

There was something else, too. She must have already had that slip of paper written out before I ever went up to talk to her at the ticket booth, because I would have noticed if she'd done it while we were sitting together at the picnic table. That meant she must have planned the whole thing ahead of time, before we even met.

Justin likes to say that things are not always what they seem to be, and in this case I was definitely willing to go along with *that.* On the surface, it looked like a boy and a girl ran into each other by chance at the fair, and then shared some food and a quick kiss before they went home. Nothing very unusual about that, especially if she made it look like we already knew each other. I wondered now if that's what all the arm-holding and sitting close together and all that jazz was supposed to be for. . . so the kiss wouldn't seem out of place, if anybody was watching us.

But why would anybody go to that much trouble? It didn't seem worth it, if all she wanted was to warn me about the wolves and slip that phone number in my hand. It seemed like it would have been a lot easier just to call me or send me a letter, instead of going for all that cloak and dagger stuff.

I looked at the crumpled slip of paper in my hand and thought about how utterly insane it all was, but one thing was for certain.

I had to see her again.

* * * * * * *

We got home maybe an hour later, and slipped indoors without a peep. Justin and Eileen were already in bed by then and we didn't want to wake them up. They were having a baby in December, and Eileen always seemed tired nowadays and couldn't sleep very well.

Cameron knew all that as well as I did, but I guess he couldn't resist teasing me, even if it did make some noise.

"So when are you bringing your girlfriend home to meet Justin and Eileen?" he asked in a hushed voice, like it was something I might not want them to overhear.

"She's not my girlfriend," I said tiredly.

"Really? It sure looked that way when y'all were smooching all over each other tonight," he laughed.

"Oh, shut up, Cam. You don't know anything about it," I said, half embarrassed and half irritated. I love Cameron to death and we're as close as two brothers could ever be, but I have to admit he can also be the most aggravating person you ever imagined.

"Sure thing, bubba. I'll shut up and let you daydream about her in peace," he said.

I groaned and rolled my eyes. He was impossible sometimes.

"Look, there's more to it than you think," I said carefully, when we got to our room and shut the door.

"I knew it! So when are you getting married, then?" he joked.

"Cameron, I'm serious. Stop it with the stupid jokes and listen to me," I said. That sobered him up a little bit.

"Okay, then. What's up, Zach?" he asked, without even a smile.

"She only kissed me so she could get close enough to whisper in my ear," I said.

That was the wrong thing to say, because Cam started to smile again and I knew he was getting ready to hit me with another zinger about my so-called girlfriend. Then he saw the look on my face, and the smile faded.

"I'm guessing she said something besides how much she loves her sweet little Zach, huh?" he said.

"Yeah, you could say that," I said dryly.

"So what was it?" he asked.

"I don't understand what she said. She told me there was somebody watching us at the fair tonight and she thought it was a werewolf," I told him.

"Huh?" he said, and the look of surprise on his face was almost enough to make me laugh, if things hadn't been so serious.

"Yeah, that's what I said, too," I agreed.

"But why would they be watching *her?* Or even us for that matter? Who is she?" he demanded.

"I don't know, Cam. I only know what she told me, and now you know as much about it as I do," I reminded him.

"That's all she said?" he asked.

"Yeah, pretty much. She said it was dangerous and to make it look good when I kissed her, so nobody would think it was a serious discussion if they saw us talking," I said.

"Dangerous how? And for who, you or her?" he asked.

"She didn't say. But if she went to that much trouble to make it look like I was just a boy she was flirting with at the fair, then it's probably nothin' to laugh at," I pointed out.

"That's crazy," he said.

"May be. I'm clueless," I told him, and he furrowed his brows and thought for a minute.

"Well, I can't think of any good reason why the wolves would care about you and me anymore. We're done with all that. So even if they *are* watching us for some unknown reason, they'll surely get tired of it after a while when they find out there's nothing to see. It'll never amount to anything, Zach," he finally said, hopefully.

I tried to tell myself he was right and there was nothing to worry about, but deep down I wasn't so sure. People don't do things for no reason, and I didn't think it was very wise to just blow it off that way.

But Cameron very clearly didn't want to hear that, and I can't say I blamed him; not after everything that happened last time we tangled with the wolves. He was happy with his life, for probably the first time he could ever remember, and he didn't want anything to mess that up. I understood him better than he thought I did, sometimes.

I wasn't real anxious to open up a whole new can of worms either, for that matter, but I had an uneasy feeling in the pit of my stomach that there might be trouble coming, and I knew it wouldn't go away just because I wished it would. I don't think I worry for nothing, but I don't shut my eyes to things I don't like, either.

I decided it wasn't the time to argue about it, though. It was late, and both of us were too sleepy to care about much of anything except going to bed at that point. I could wait and see what Jolie had to say when I called her tomorrow, and then if it seemed important enough I could sit down and try to make Cameron listen.

"I don't know. Maybe you're right," I finally said.

"Sure I am. Don't worry about it," he agreed, and that was all we said about it that night.

I was antsy all day long at school the next day. I kept playing with that slip of paper with Jolie's phone number on it and thinking about what to say when I called her. I couldn't focus on my work or pay attention to anything else; I thought three o'clock would never come.

Me and Cameron both had baseball practice after school that day, but I decided it probably wouldn't hurt me to miss it for once, much as I hated to.

The city was offering a fall baseball league that year, like they sometimes do, and that's why we were having off-season practice like that. Me and Cam always used to sit around at school with our best friends James and Levi to talk about playing for the Texas Rangers someday, believe it or not, and all four of us signed up for Fall Ball because we knew we needed all the practice we could get. Maybe it sounds like a wild and crazy dream that'll never happen, but hey, you never know. I won an All-Star trophy last summer during the regular season, and I don't think I've ever been prouder of anything in my life. So. . . we'll see.

But in spite of all that, what I really wanted more than anything right then was to call Jolie and get some answers. Practice could wait. I had Cameron drop me off at home before he drove to the ball field, and as soon as he was out of sight, I pulled out my phone.

She answered on the first ring.

"Hello?" she said.

"Hey, it's. . ." I started, but she cut me off before I could get another word in.

"Meet me at the soccer field at Spring Lake Park in half an hour," she said quickly, and hung up on me.

I looked at the phone for a second. How did she think I was supposed to get to the soccer field? Flap my wings and fly? That was all the way across town, and Cam had the truck.

I muttered something under my breath about rude girls who expected too much, and then I called a taxi to take me down there. It was the only thing I could think of on such short notice, even though it cost me twenty bucks that I couldn't really spare. I might have been more annoyed, if I hadn't still been dying of curiosity.

Anyway, it took longer than thirty minutes for me to get to the soccer field; more like forty-five, to tell the truth. Some little kids were playing a game on the field itself when I got there, and Jolie was nowhere to be seen.

I finally found her sitting on a bench under an oak tree, watching the kids play. I almost didn't recognize her at first because she was wearing a green scarf that covered her hair and some big black sunglasses that made it hard to see her face very well. But when I got close enough, I knew it was her.

I sat down on the bench beside her without saying anything, and she took off the sunglasses and turned to look at me.

"You're kinda late, boy," she said mildly. That aggravated the tar out of me, but I bit my tongue and didn't say so.

"I got here as soon as I could," I told her.

"Well, I don't guess it matters. We're both here now," she agreed.

"Don't you think you should tell me what's going on now?" I told her.

"Yeah, but not here. I don't think anybody's trailing me today, but you can never be totally sure. Come on," she said, standing up.

I got up too, and she headed for the parking lot at a brisk walk. I had to trot to keep up with her.

She led me to a brand new banana yellow Volkswagen Beetle and unlocked the doors. The windows were tinted so dark they looked like black mirrors, and she had a Louisiana license plate that said "SMOKIN".

That made me want to laugh, and when I thought about it for little while, I decided maybe that was the whole idea behind it. She was poking fun at herself in a subtle kind of way, like she knew she was pretty but didn't take herself too seriously because of it. I kinda liked her for that.

I got in the passenger seat without saying anything, though, and she drove out of the park.

"Where are we going?" I asked.

"Nowhere, really. We're just driving so we can talk without anybody hearing what I have to tell you," she said.

"You couldn't tell me on the phone?" I pointed out.

"Nope. Anybody can pick up cell phone calls. Not secure enough," she said.

I wondered why anybody would care enough to try, but I shook my head and let it go.

"Okay, so tell me. I'm all ears," I said.

"All right, Zach, I'll get right to the point. I know what you and Cameron did with the Trewick pod two years ago, and there are some things I'd like to ask you about that," she began.

"Pod?" I asked.

"Yeah. You know, a flock of birds, a herd of cows. A pod of werewolves," she said, and I wanted to laugh again.

"That's silly," I told her.

"Maybe so, but that's the word. Better not think they're silly, though," she said. That reminded me of what happened in Tennessee at my mom and dad's place, and I didn't feel like laughing anymore after that.

"Yeah, you're right about that," I admitted.

"Anyway, it was good work. I'm impressed," she told me.

"Uh, thanks, I guess," I said, wondering all over again who she was and how she knew so much.

"You're welcome. But like I said, there are some things I'd like to ask you," she repeated.

"Yeah, there are some things I'd like to know, too," I told her.

"All right, then. I tell you what; you tell me something I want to know, and then I'll tell you something you want to know. We'll take turns. Deal?" she asked.

"Fair enough," I agreed.

"Okay, then. First question: How did you destroy those wolf stones?" she asked.

"We had some help. There used to be a spring of holy water not far from here, and if you sprinkled some of it on one of the stones and prayed over it, then it broke the curse," I explained.

"There *used* to be?" she asked.

"Yeah, the wolves found it not long after we did, and they blew it up with dynamite. We barely had enough to finish," I told her.

"I see," she said, half to herself.

"Okay, my turn to ask a question. Who are you, really, and what have you got to do with all this?" I asked.

"Well, you already know my name. That's who I really am. And as for what I've got to do with all this. . . I'm a professional werewolf hunter," she said, without a trace of a smile.

"Does that pay pretty well?" I asked her dryly.

"A lot better than flipping burgers after school," she said, equally dryly.

I had to laugh.

"How do you get involved with something like that?" I asked. I couldn't help wondering, you know. It's not like they could put an ad in the paper.

"Oh, it's the family business, you might say. We've been doing it for centuries. We fight the wolves wherever we find them, however we can, but there are always more pods popping up out there," she explained.

"*More* pods?" I asked, not liking what I was hearing.

"Surely you didn't think there was just one pod in the whole world, did you?" she asked. I remembered wondering about that very thing a few times, now that she mentioned it, but it never seemed very important before. Not till now.

"How many pods are there?" I asked grimly.

"I'm not sure, total. I know of at least ten right this minute. There's one in New Mexico, and another one in Wisconsin, and a third one in Ohio. I know of others in England and France and Australia and. . ."

"Okay, I get it," I interrupted, a little bit sourly this time. She was making me feel like I hadn't accomplished anything at all by stamping out just one pod.

"No need to be tetchy," she scolded.

"Sorry," I said.

"In any case, my turn now. I know you grew up in a pod, so how come you decided not to join them?" she said. That was a harder question than the first one, and I had to think about it for a minute to give her a good answer.

"Well. . . I was only twelve when I ran away, you know. At the time I wasn't even totally sure why, except I knew I didn't want to be a monster. I think I could always tell they didn't really want me, you know, and maybe that's why I started to look somewhere else," I said.

"What made you think they didn't want you?" she asked.

"Because there was an old tradition they had, about how the seventh-generation boy with blue eyes was supposed to be the Curse Breaker and destroy all the *loup-garous*. I fit the description, so I guess they didn't like that very much. Cam did too, and they never could make up their minds which one of us it was," I explained.

"Interesting. So where did that tradition come from? Any idea?" she asked.

"Yeah, Cam knows more about it than I do because he was with them longer, but he told me it was something Daniel Trewick said; the one who started our pod," I told her.

"That makes sense. Pod leaders tend to know things like that. Most of them are way too curious for their own good; that's usually what gets them in trouble in the first place," she agreed, nodding.

"All right, my turn now. Where do those wolf-stones come from in the first place? Why is it only certain ones that work?" I asked. That was one of the things Daniel Trewick never mentioned in his journal, and the five stones for that pod had been scattered out in such weird and far-flung places, I couldn't help being curious.

"Oh, that's no big secret. Whenever somebody wants to form a new pod, they take some dust from Mont Mouchet in France, and they sprinkle it on a piece of sandstone somewhere in the right sort of place, curse it with certain ceremonies, and then they're in business. It's not very hard, actually, if you know how." she told me.

"Okay, but why choose places so far apart? My pod had five stones, scattered out everywhere from Tennessee to Texas. Why just those and no others?" I asked, and Jolie shrugged.

"There's no telling about that part. Your pod leader picked them for some reason. Maybe he traveled a lot and decided to curse every stone he came across that looked like the right kind, or maybe he just found several old ones that other pods didn't use anymore. That happens sometimes, too," she said.

"So what's the right kind of stone?" I asked.

"I don't remember *all* the rules; I know it has to do with the rock formations in the area, and it can't be cracked, and there are a couple of other things, I think," she said.

"But if somebody does find the right kind, all they have to do is sprinkle it with that dust from Mount Moosejaw or wherever it is, and that's it?" I asked.

"Mont Mouchet," she corrected, "and yes, that's pretty much it. That and speak the curse. That's how most new pods are formed, although like I said, now and then you get one where somebody finds an old stone from another pod and figures out how to use it. That's kinda rare, though," she said.

"So what if somebody destroyed that mountain?" I asked.

"Nice idea, but it's a *mountain,* Zach. You can't destroy a whole mountain," she said.

"Well. . . no, maybe not," I admitted.

"All right. My turn, and last question," she said solemnly.

"Go for it," I said.

"How would you like to be a werewolf hunter?" she asked. I have to admit, that one caught me totally flat-footed.

"Huh?" I asked, not sure I heard her right.

"You heard me. We always need some good recruits," she said.

"I thought you said it was just a family business," I reminded her.

"Yeah, it is, but we do make exceptions now and then, for the right person," she told me.

I felt a thrill of excitement at the thought; I won't deny that, and I wanted to say yes like I'd never wanted anything else in my life before. There are certain things that touch your heart instantly and make you thirst after them like water on a hot day, you know. That's what it felt like.

But then on the other hand, I remembered how Cam almost died, last time we got involved with something like that. The danger to people I loved was very real, and this time there wouldn't be any sweet water to save them if anything went wrong.

"I'd have to think about that for a while," I finally said, reluctantly.

"Yeah, I thought you probably would. Here's my card, whenever you make up your mind," she said.

And believe it or not, she handed me a hot pink business card with shiny red letters that said *Jolie Doucet, Werewolf Hunter,* with her cell phone number down at the bottom. It was surreal. I guessed she was a Cajun, with a French last name like that, although you wouldn't have guessed it by looking at her. Most Cajuns have dark hair.

I stuck the card in my pocket without thinking too much about it.

"I'll have to let you off somewhere downtown, if that's okay. Like I said, I don't think anybody was trailing me today, but you can never be totally sure. It might not be safe for you if one of the wolves saw us together, especially not close to your house; some of them are mean customers," she said.

"Why are they following you all the time, anyway?" I asked.

"There's such a thing as revenge, Zach," she said cryptically, with a sad sort of smile.

That shut me up from asking any more questions for a while; I wasn't sure I wanted to know the answers.

She pulled in at the south end of the mall and parked the car, then turned to look at me.

"Think about it for a while before you make up your mind, Zach. We could do a lot together, you and me," she said.

There was a long pause, and then she did something I wasn't expecting. She lifted her hand to my cheek, and trailed her fingers across the bit of golden stubble I was just starting to grow. It tickled, and the way she did it was almost shy, like she wasn't sure what I might think.

"Call me sometime anyway, Blue-Eyes, if you want to," she said, and all I could do was nod. I'm not usually that tongue-tied, but for once I seemed to have forgotten how to speak.

I stood there in the parking lot and watched her drive away until she disappeared amongst the traffic on Richmond Road, and then I slowly raised one hand to my face. I swear my skin still tingled where her fingers had touched.

My thoughts were too confused at that moment to even begin to write them all down, so I won't try. But one thing was certain: she'd given me an *awful* lot to chew on.

I glanced at my watch and saw that it was only four-thirty, so that meant I was stuck downtown for at least an hour before anybody could come get me. Cam would still be at baseball practice for another thirty minutes, and Justin and Eileen wouldn't be off work till then, either. There was nobody else I could call for a ride, and I didn't have enough money for another taxi.

I didn't mind so much, though. I walked over to Books-A-Million and browsed the shelves for a while, just to see if there was anything new and interesting. I love that place. There's always something I haven't seen before, and they don't mind if you pull up a chair and read for a while. It's like a huge library with books about anything you could imagine, and if you like something especially well you can always buy it. What could be better?

I went to the section that has books about werewolves and such things, and found one that was called *Hunters of the Night: Real-Life Tales of Monster Slayers.* It sounded cheesy, but Jolie had me interested in the subject and I had nothing better to do at the moment.

I didn't really study it all that close, just flipped through the pages and read whatever caught my eye for a second. But there was nothing about Mont Mouchet, or *loup-garous,* or even Cajun werewolf hunters with flaming red hair.

I still wasn't sure what to think about what she said; *either* part of it. The idea of becoming a werewolf hunter myself was a huge thing to think about, but even that was *nothing* compared to the thought that she might really like me.

Yeah, yeah, I know; roll your eyes and laugh at me if you want to, but what can I say? She was beautiful and interesting and even funny sometimes, and it's not every day that you meet somebody like that, you know. I'm no more immune to a pretty face than anybody else is.

I couldn't help wondering *why* she liked me so much, though. Jolie was beautiful enough to take her pick of almost any boy she wanted. I've been told a few times that I'm cute, it's true, but I don't measure up to *that* level and I knew it as well as anybody. We hadn't talked long enough for her to be all that impressed with my warm and loving heart, either. So if it wasn't my insides and it wasn't my outsides, then what could it be?

It always makes me uneasy when things don't add up, you know. It means there's something missing from the way I'm trying to understand the world. It crossed my mind that Jolie was smart enough to *pretend* she liked me for her own purposes without meaning it; that's what she did at the fair that night, after all.

But nevertheless, I won't lie about it; I kinda hoped she really meant it this time and that we could talk and get to know each other better, regardless of what happened with the werewolf hunting thing.

It was after five o'clock by then, so I called Justin to pick me up on his way home from work. He did, and by the time I got home Cam was there too.

"I thought you stayed home today," he said when I saw him.

"Yeah, I decided to go to the bookstore for a while, that's all," I said.

I was kinda shy about telling him what happened with Jolie that afternoon. I knew he wouldn't like the werewolf part, and I could just imagine what he'd say if I told him about her touching my cheek; I'd never hear the end of it if he ever sunk his teeth into *that* juicy little tidbit.

But he didn't ask about her, surprisingly enough.

"So how was practice today?" I asked, mostly to turn the conversation to something else.

"Oh, it was okay. Jake hit a ball all the way over the back fence and we lost it in the ravine," he told me.

"Seriously? Jake never hits anything," I said, mildly curious. Jake was what you might call the team mascot, more than anything else. He was the kind of kid who'd trip over his own feet if they weren't attached to his legs. Sometimes even then, actually.

"Yeah, he really did. I saw him do it," Cameron said.

"I almost wish I'd been there, now. That's the kind of thing you don't see every day," I said.

"For sure," Cam agreed.

I didn't think any more about it right then. At the time, Jake's home run just seemed like a passing curiosity, here today and forgotten tomorrow. Before long I'd have good reason to think a lot about it and what it meant. But for the time being I was still blissfully unaware.

Chapter Two

I thought a lot about everything for the next few days; in fact, I think it's safe to say I hardly thought about anything else. I was so distracted at baseball practice on Thursday afternoon that I got bonked on the head with a flyball, and I'm *never* like that. I remember even James asked me what was on my mind, and he's not exactly the sharpest knife in the drawer when it comes to noticing that kind of thing.

It was several things. I kept remembering that kiss at the fair, and the way Jolie touched my face and asked me to call her, and even that silly SMOKIN license plate that made me laugh; I chewed endlessly over what it all meant and whether she really liked me or whether she had some other plan up her sleeve. It was driving me crazy.

But it wasn't only that. I was starting to worry about the whole werewolf hunting thing, too. Yeah, at first it thrilled me like nothing I ever felt before, but after a while I figured out why that was. Jolie had just finished telling me about all these pods that still existed, which meant the Curse was still very much alive, and then right in the middle of my disappointment she handed me what seemed like a second chance to break the thing. That was a powerful lure, you know. Especially for me, the one who was supposed to be the Curse-Breaker. *That's* why it touched such a deep place in my heart and set me on fire the way it did. When God gives you work to do, it's not something you can forget about so easily.

But the more I thought about it, the less certain I was that Jolie was offering me anything even remotely like that. She wanted help fighting wolves, and that wasn't quite the same thing. In fact, I couldn't help but wonder what it was that a werewolf hunter *did,* exactly.

Did it mean she carried a box of silver bullets in her pocket and a pistol in her purse, and that she hunted werewolves the same way some people hunt deer? That's kinda what it *sounded* like it meant, and that was an awfully dark and gruesome thought, you know. There was no way I wanted to get involved with something like *that.* I wasn't even sure I wanted to talk to somebody who was, no matter how beautiful and interesting she might be.

Maybe I was tying myself up in knots over nothing, and I guess the smartest thing to do would have been to call her up and just ask her about all that stuff, of course. But that's where the whole does-she-like-me thing came back into play again; I was afraid to say the wrong thing and make her mad at me, or even worse, laugh at me. Girls who are that pretty can be hard to talk to even at the best of times, believe it or not, and this was light years from the best and easiest of times.

So I dithered and dawdled and put off calling her while I tried to sort it all out inside.

Saturday morning I went out to Red Lick like I usually do, to mow Miss Edith's grass and do whatever else she might need done around the house. She was almost a hundred years old and she wasn't up to that kind of thing anymore.

I liked my visits out there. She always made me tea and cookies, or "sweet biscuits" as she sometimes called them, and usually we sat and talked for a while on the verandah after I was done with everything.

That particular Saturday started out pretty much like usual. I got to her house about nine o'clock and weeded the front flower beds, then repainted the trim on the garage with dark green paint.

I got done with all that about three o'clock, and then I sat down on the verandah to cool off a bit before I headed home. Miss Edith brought out the tea in a glass pitcher full of ice, and some sugar cookies on a lace platter cover.

You shouldn't think that was anything unusual, though. She always used to tell me it was the little things that mattered most, and you should always make your guests feel like royalty, no matter who they might be. She was one of those gracious old Southern ladies, and that's just the way she did things. I loved her to death, but there was always a certain level of good manners you had to maintain at her house, too.

So I sat there in my white wicker chair and I was careful to eat politely and not just wolf down my food like I might do at home.

"Zachary, you seem a little bit distracted today. Is there something on your mind?" she asked me that afternoon. She always used my full name like that for some reason, but I was used to it by then.

"No, Miss Edith, but I met this girl at the fair a few days ago and I guess I've been thinking about her a lot," I admitted. She smiled.

"Oh, I see. Well tell me all about her!" she said.

"Her name is Jolie, and she's got red hair and she's from somewhere down in Louisiana. Nackadish or something like that," I said.

"Do you mean Natchitoches?" she asked.

"Yes, that's it," I agreed.

"I take it you like her, then?" she asked.

I couldn't help thinking again about the whole werewolf hunting thing, and maybe I hesitated just a bit too long before I answered.

"Yes, ma'am, I really do. She's a lot of fun to be around," I finally said.

"Hmm. . . You don't seem too sure of yourself when you say that, Zachary. Is there something about her that bothers you?" she asked. Miss Edith is a wonderful person to talk to about most anything, and I decided it couldn't hurt to see what she thought.

"It's not exactly that. It's just that she does some things I'm not sure I like, that's all," I said.

"Care to tell me about it?" she asked.

"Well. . . she says the world is full of other werewolves besides just that one group me and Cameron had to deal with, and she says she's a werewolf hunter," I said.

"Which means?" she asked.

"I'm not sure. I guess it means she kills them. I didn't think to ask her about that part," I admitted.

"It seems strange that such a person would meet you by accident at the fair, don't you think?" she pointed out.

"Oh, no, it wasn't an accident. She came looking for me because she wanted to ask me some questions and offer me a job as a werewolf hunter, too," I explained.

"And what did you tell her?" she asked.

"I told her I'd have to think about it for a while," I said.

"But you wanted to say yes?" she prodded.

"Maybe if I knew for sure it wasn't anything bad. But even then I'm not sure. I want to break the Curse, not fight wolves forever. Besides that, I know Cam wouldn't be happy about getting wrapped up in something like that again. I'm not even sure Justin and Eileen would be very pleased right now, not with the baby coming so soon. I know it puts them all in danger, at least a little bit. It's just that I feel like we didn't finish the job we were supposed to do, if there are still all these pods out there. So if I had a chance to finish it now, then don't you think I ought to try?" I asked her.

Miss Edith didn't answer at first, just took off her gold-rimmed spectacles and polished them on the hem of her dress.

"You're a good boy, Zachary. You already know the answer to that question without me needing to tell you, don't you?" she asked.

"Yes, ma'am, I guess I probably do, and maybe working with Jolie is a good way to get started. It just bothers me the way her family is going about it, if they're really killing folks. What the wolves are doing is evil, but that doesn't mean it's right to go after them with silver bullets, either. They're still people, aren't they?" I asked, hesitantly. It was hard to put into words exactly what I felt.

Miss Edith smiled again.

"Oh, indeed they are. I'm glad to see you can still remember that, and think of them that way," she said.

"Love the sinner, hate the sin," I said weakly. I meant it as a joke, but Miss Edith took me seriously.

"Exactly!" she cried, "Always remember that, and you'll never become a hard and cruel man."

"I try," I said, half to myself. Miss Edith looked at me long and searchingly for a minute, and then she seemed to reach some kind of decision.

"Come with me, Zachary. There's something I want to show you," she went on.

I got up from my seat and followed her inside. She walked slowly, so it wasn't hard to keep up with her. She crossed the dining room and took a key from under a white ceramic cat on a shelf, then used it to unlock the cellar door. I'd never been down there before, so I was a little bit curious about what it was she wanted to show me.

She took her time going down the stairs, holding on to the railing carefully to keep from falling. When we got to the bottom she pulled a string to switch on a single dusty light bulb that didn't do much at all to light up the place.

It turned out to be a wine cellar. There were three of those wooden shelves that hold wine bottles, all of them stacked full, and that was about it.

I was disappointed, to tell the truth. I'd been expecting something a little more interesting than that. Miss Edith went slowly to the closest shelf, pulled out a dusty green bottle, and then handed it to me.

I dusted cobwebs off the label, which was something French and dated for 1965. I don't know much about wine, but I did remember that older is supposed to be better. 1965 was pretty old, so I guessed it was a fairly valuable bottle, if it came to that.

"Taste of it," Miss Edith said.

"Huh?" I said, totally forgetting my manners for a second in shock. Miss Edith was not at all the kind of person I would have expected to offer me alcohol.

"Don't grunt, Zachary; you're not a pig," she scolded me, "Now do as I say, and taste of it."

I glanced at Miss Edith out of the corner of my eye, just to see if she was really serious. She certainly looked that way, and I figured one sip of wine wouldn't kill me, after all. I popped the cork out and lifted the bottle to my lips, and then I took a small drink.

It wasn't wine.

It was water, with a faint taste of honeysuckle blossoms.

My eyes widened, and I looked at Miss Edith again. She was watching me, with a smile on her face.

"Always plan ahead, Zachary. I filled up these bottles for years, whenever I went out to the spring. Now it's gone, but these are still here. There are about two hundred bottles full, more or less. I've never told anyone else on earth about this place, except you," she said.

"So why are you telling *me*?" I asked, too stunned to think of anything else to say.

"I have good reason, Zachary. I've been wanting to tell you for a long time, but I needed to see what kind of boy you'd turn out to be, first. But I've known you for two years now, and we've talked about all kinds of things, and I believe you're the one I should leave it to," she said.

"Leave it to?" I repeated.

"I'm ninety-nine years old, Zachary. I won't be here much longer. But I couldn't trust all this to a stranger. It matters too much. I hoped and prayed that God would send me someone who could take it up, before I had to lay it down. I believe that's you. So I'm giving it to you, child, to do with as you see fit. All I can tell you is to use it wisely, and never tell anyone you have it. Not even your best friends," she said.

"Miss Edith. . . " I began, but she laid a finger on my lips to shush me.

"Hush, Zachary. My grandfather told me the secret and left me this place when he died in 1932, and I've kept it faithfully all these years. Now I'm asking you to do the same thing. There's no spring to guard anymore, but that only makes this place all the more precious. Use it wisely and use it well," she repeated.

I went home that afternoon lost in thought, and for a while I even managed to forget about Jolie, believe it or not. I was thrilled to find out there was a secret stash of sweet water somewhere when I'd thought it was all used or destroyed, and that cast a whole new light on the question of what I should do about the wolves.

I took it as a sign, for one thing. I don't believe in accidents, you know; not when it comes to things like that. I knew the water was a miracle, meant to be used to break the Curse. So if the Curse was still around, then it didn't surprise me that God made sure there was enough water left to finish the job He meant it for. No werewolf could frustrate that plan, not even with dynamite, and maybe at the same time He was encouraging me to remember that I was still the Curse-Breaker and my work wasn't done yet.

That was all fine and well, as far as it went. But at the same time, there had to be some other purpose for the water than just breaking wolf-stones like I did before. I could never finish all of them that way, not even with two hundred bottles full; not as long as people could keep going to Mont Mouchet and forming new ones. There had to be something else it was meant for than just that. If I could only figure out what it was.

It changed the way I looked at the werewolf hunting issue, too. In fact I was tempted to call Jolie right then and tell her I'd decided to take her up on the offer, as long as I didn't have to kill anybody. It seemed to have come along at exactly the right time, and I didn't think that was an accident, either. *She* might not think of the job as a stepping stone to breaking the Curse, but that didn't mean I couldn't use it that way.

I still had to wonder about the personal stuff, of course; whether she really liked me or not, and what I thought about it even if she did. That mattered, too, but I figured if we were working together we could sort out all that when there was time.

"How was Miss Edith today?" Eileen asked me when I walked in the door.

"Oh, she was fine," I said, still lost in thought.

"Something came in the mail for you this morning, Zach," she said.

"Really? What is it?" I asked her, mildly curious. I don't often get any mail, so whenever I did it was always interesting.

"Here it is," she said, handing me a pale pink envelope. It was addressed to me, sure enough, but there was no return address on it at all. The postmark was from Natchitoches, Louisiana, three days ago. When I saw that, I knew it had to be from Jolie; she was the only person I knew from down there.

I moseyed out to the barn and sat down on the bench beside Buster's stall to read it, just to have some privacy. I like to go out there sometimes when I want to be alone, or if I want to talk to somebody without worrying what they might think. Horses are good listeners, you know. They just turn their ears around in your direction and take in whatever you're saying, and they hardly ever talk back.

Nobody else was out there, so I opened my letter and started to read. The paper was pink, too, and it smelled like wild cherries.

Hey Blue-Eyes,

I hope everything is okay with you. I forgot to tell you I'll be back at my Aunt Angie's house this weekend, and I thought we might get together and have lunch sometime or maybe go see a movie if you want to. Here's her number, just in case. See you soon!

Jolie Doucet

She ended the letter with a bunch of x's and o's, and I smiled a little when I saw that. Eileen told me once that those are supposed to mean "hugs and kisses", which I never would have guessed if she hadn't told me. I always used to think they were just some meaningless doodly thing that girls like to put on letters for some reason, the same way they draw hearts and butterflies and flowers on everything they can get their hands on.

I still didn't think it meant *that* much, honestly, but nevertheless it made me feel warm right down to my toenails, cheesy as that sounds. It's amazing how a little slip of cherry-scented paper can do that, isn't it?

Anyway, I decided it was an excellent time to go ahead and call her. She ought to be at her aunt's house already, if the letter was right, and I had more than half a mind to ask her if she wanted to go have some ice cream and see a movie. It was still plenty early enough. We could talk, and she could explain exactly what it meant to be a werewolf hunter, and then if all went well I was ready to tell her I'd take the job. Everything else could wait till later.

I saved her aunt's number in my phone so I wouldn't lose it, and then I pushed the call button.

It didn't go through. Instead, all I got was a recorded message telling me the number was out of order. I tried it again just to make sure I hadn't made a mistake, and when it still didn't work I tried the number on the business card she gave me. That one went straight to her voicemail.

I furrowed my brow in disappointment and kinda wondered if maybe something was wrong. Surely she wouldn't ask me twice to call her and then not answer the phone, would she? She had to know it was me; she'd have caller ID on her cell phone even if her aunt didn't have it at home.

Maybe any other time I would have just shrugged it off and tried again in a day or two, and that's what I almost did even now. But I couldn't help remembering all that stuff she said about the wolves following her around and wanting revenge, you know. That put a little bit different twist on things, so I sat there and chewed my bottom lip for a while, trying to make up my mind what to do.

I finally decided it was worthwhile to drive over to her aunt's house for a minute, just to make sure everything was all right. So I called information and got the address that went with the number: 933 Ash Street. I knew vaguely where that was; somewhere downtown near the post office, if I remembered right.

Justin gave me and Cam his old Dodge Ram 4x4 when he bought a new one last year, and most of the time we don't fight much about who gets to drive it and when and where. It's our pet project, and it spends about as much time parked under the hickory tree behind the house as it does anywhere else. We bought some chrome wheels and bed rails for it, and a glass pack muffler that makes it just loud enough to sound mean when you step on the gas.

We had plans to get a cold-air intake and some other stuff like that, when we had the money. Justin says neither one of us can have a job except on Saturdays or during the summer, so it's hard to rake up the cash for those kinds of things. Especially for me, since I was always at Red Lick on Saturdays, doing stuff for Miss Edith.

Anyway, the keys were hanging on the wall next to the front door, so I went in there intending to take them and go.

"Going somewhere?" Cam asked. He was sitting on the couch watching a movie and looked up when I opened the door.

"Yeah, just downtown for a minute. I'll be right back," I said.

"Mind if I come along?" he asked.

That put me in an awkward position, because of course I really didn't want *anybody* to come with me, but it was hard for me to say so.

"Sure, I guess," I said grudgingly. If I had to, I could come up with some excuse for stopping at the house on Ash Street. Cam probably wouldn't quiz me too much.

So we hopped in the truck and drove down there, and I went to the post office first, since I had to come up with another reason for going downtown than just to check on Jolie.

"Eileen already checked the mail this morning," Cameron said when we got there.

"Did she?" I asked.

"You know she did, Zach. You got that pink letter today," he reminded me.

I hadn't known he knew about that, but then of course you can't keep secrets very well when you live with somebody. He must have seen it on the kitchen table earlier.

"Yeah, I guess I forgot about that," I lied, and Cam laughed at me.

"No you didn't, Zach. I saw you go out to the barn with that letter in your hand and then as soon as you came back in, you wanted to come down here. That's why I wanted to come, so I could see what was up. So whatever it is, you might as well spill it," he said.

I sighed.

"All right. But if I tell you then no laughing about it, Cam," I told him.

"Okay, that's fine," he agreed.

"I wanted to stop by Jolie's aunt's house and check on her, just to make sure she's all right," I said.

"Really? Why wouldn't she be, and why do you care, and what do you think you could do about it anyway?" he asked.

All tough questions.

"Well. . . that pink letter was from her. She said she'd be in town this weekend and she asked me to call her so we could maybe go do something together; that's all." I said.

"And?" he asked.

"So I called her and I keep getting a message that says the number is out of order. It's probably nothing, but I just want to go check it out since it's not that far anyway," I explained.

"So you *do* like her. I knew it all along," he smiled.

"Cam, you promised. No laughing," I reminded him.

"Oh, all right; I won't. I just think it's sweet, that's all," he said. I wasn't exactly sure what *that* was supposed to mean, but I knew better than to ask him about it. If I did, that would just keep the whole topic alive for that much longer. So I didn't take the bait.

"Okay, let's go down to the old lady's house and see what's up," he said after a while.

Ash Street was only a couple of blocks from the post office, just like I thought, and as soon as we found it we drove slowly north, counting house numbers.

Before long we came to a black mailbox with 933 on it, and that's when we got a nasty surprise. The house was a burned-out wreck. All the windows were busted out and the front door was gone, and there was black soot and smoke stains everywhere. There was nothing left but a gutted ruin.

No doubt that was why the phone number didn't work. It looked awfully recent, too; the place was even still smoking a little bit, here and there. Besides that, Jolie wouldn't have been talking about staying here for the weekend, if she knew it was burned down. That meant it couldn't have happened more than three days ago at the most.

"Are you sure this is the place, Zach?" Cam asked me.

"Yeah, it has to be. This is the right address, and there are no other houses close to this one. Let's take a closer look and make sure, though," I said.

We got out of the truck and slowly picked our way up the concrete walkway and onto the steps.

"Look, here's the 933," I said when we got closer, pointing to the metal numbers that were still attached next to the missing front door. I wondered what had happened.

Oh, I know it was a house fire, of course; I'm not stupid. What I meant was, I wondered if maybe it was more than just an accident. Maybe one of the wolves had spotted Jolie while she was there and then torched the place on purpose.

There was a string of that yellow plastic *"Do Not Cross"* tape wrapped around the house to keep people from going inside, but I ignored that and ducked underneath it.

"What are you doing, Zach? You want to get arrested?" Cameron hissed at me.

"I just want to look, that's all. Go wait for me in the truck if you want to, or else come in here yourself and then nobody can see us," I told him.

He must have decided he couldn't change my mind, because he followed me inside without saying anything else about it.

There wasn't much to be seen in there, at first glance. Just burned and scorched furniture, covered in black soot and still soaking wet from the fire hoses. It stank like you wouldn't believe.

But there *was* a half-melted computer sitting on a desk against the wall, and I decided that was worth looking at first. I couldn't possibly do any more damage to it than there already was, so I tore the cover off the tower part and rooted around inside until I found the hard drive. It didn't seem to be damaged, but after going through that much heat you could never tell for sure. I disconnected it from what was left of the CPU and slipped it in my pocket.

"What's that for?" Cam asked.

"Just curious. Might find out something, if it still works," I said.

We took a quick look around the rest of the house and didn't find anything else worth mentioning. Fire is really good at destroying things, you know.

I was uneasy about spending too much time in the house because, like Cameron pointed out, they put up that yellow tape for a reason, and you can get in trouble for crossing it when you're not supposed to. And besides that, burnt-out houses are dangerous places to be. You never know when the floor might cave in or the ceiling might collapse on your head, and there's broken glass and rusty nails everywhere.

As soon as we glanced at everything, we got out of there. We were both smudged with greasy black soot and stank to high heaven just from the short time we'd been inside.

"Do you really want to get in the truck like this? It'll stink for a week," Cam pointed out.

"No, but I think it'll be okay if we throw somethin' over the seat," I said. I looked in the bed to see if there was a tarp or a blanket or anything like that. There usually would have been, but apparently not today.

"Never mind. We'll just have to clean it out real good," I said.

As soon as we got back home, that's exactly what we did while we still had some daylight left. We wiped down the seats and sprayed them with Febreeze and put a can of Eileen's French

Vanilla air freshener in there. Neither one of us especially likes that flavor; it smells like stale birthday cake to me. But it was all we could find, and it was way better than smoke and water smell.

"I guess that will have to do," I said.

"Yeah, it will. So what are you doing with that hard drive?" Cam asked.

"Watch and see," I told him.

As soon as we got back inside, I took the cover off my computer and then plugged the hard drive from the burnt computer into one of the empty slots reserved for extra internal hard drives.

You might have noticed that I really like computers. Most people don't know much about them except how to use whatever software they like, but they're amazing things and they can do wonderful stuff if you know how to play with them the right way.

Anyway, I put the cover back in place without screwing it down, and then turned everything back on. It started up as usual, and as soon as it was ready I clicked my way through to the screen where all the drives were listed. Sure enough, there was a new one there.

"Bingo," I said to myself.

I clicked on the new drive to look at the files, and of course there were tons of them. I expected that. But I didn't care about the operating system files or solitaire or any of that crud. I wanted documents or spreadsheets or databases; anything that might have useful information in it.

I soon discovered that the hard drive had been damaged pretty badly by the fire. Heat does funny things to magnetic memory, which is why they always tell you not to let your computer get too hot. That drive was chock full of corrupt files that couldn't be opened anymore, or if they could then they didn't show anything but gibberish. I'd be willing to bet that way more than half the memory was either erased or ruined.

But not all of it.

I found one file that contained what seemed to be locations of *loup-garou* pods and basic information about them. There were a lot more of them than I expected, and I was discouraged all over again about how little me and Cameron had actually done. One pod was just a drop in the bucket, it seemed.

There was also an entire folder full of in-depth case files on each pod from the list, but most of those were unreadable and the rest of them were badly damaged.

There was another file that looked like an amateur family tree and history of the Doucet family since 1767, which was apparently when they first got into werewolf hunting. That one was mostly just a list of names and dates and who was related to whom and some of the notable things they did, but in places Angie had expanded it to read like a storybook. The tail end of that one was corrupted, too, so I could only read the first few pages of it.

I guess I was so absorbed in looking at files that I forgot Cameron didn't already know about all the werewolf hunting stuff. But he's not stupid. He was looking over my shoulder when I opened that file with all the pod locations, and he knew what it meant as soon as he saw the word *loup-garou.*

"What do these people have to do with the wolves, Zach?" he asked me quietly.

There was no way to keep it a secret anymore after that, so I told him.

"Jolie and her family are werewolf hunters. She came to find us because she heard about how we destroyed all those wolf-stones, and she hoped I could help them fight some other pods," I said.

"Pods?" he asked.

"Yeah, she said that's what you call a group of werewolves. I never knew that before," I admitted.

"And what did you tell her?" he asked.

"I told her I'd have to think about it for a while; that's all," I admitted, not wanting to look him in the eye.

"I see. Well, it sure looks to me like you're doing a whole lot more than just *thinking* about it," he said, crossing his arms over his chest and starting to scowl.

"I just want to make sure she's all right, Cam. You saw that house today," I reminded him.

"Yeah, all I saw was a burnt-out house, and that could happen to anybody. She doesn't even live there," he pointed out.

"No, but it seems awfully fishy, anyway. She stays there a lot, and she kept talking about the wolves following her around and wanting to get revenge, remember?" I asked him.

Cameron thought about that for a few seconds, but if it softened his mood at all he sure didn't let it show on his face.

"I guess she didn't bother to tell you which *pod* it might be that hated her so much, did she?" he asked sarcastically.

"No, she didn't. But I'm sure a lot of them probably have grudges and scores to settle against her family. They *are* werewolf hunters, after all," I said, and Cameron shook his head sadly.

"You're getting dragged into another fight, Zach, and this one's not even yours," he said.

"I'm trying not to, Cam, but I can't let anything happen to her," I said.

"Bubba, this is not just about her and you know that as well as I do," he told me.

That was the heart of it all, right there, and we both knew it. Cameron knew I could never turn my back on breaking the Curse till it was finished. I might say I was just thinking about it, or just helping a pretty girl, but he knew me better than that. He knew my heart's desire was to crush the Curse forever, and I was a fool if I pretended not to know it myself. I was trying to help Jolie, true, but that wasn't the whole story by a long shot.

I sighed. It never feels good when somebody yanks the warm rug of make-believe out from under your feet, but it's usually

better when they do. I wasn't being completely honest with
Cameron about my plans and purposes, and he was right to call
me down for that. People will risk their lives for the truth
sometimes, but never for anything less.

"Cam, do you remember, a long time ago, when you told me
about the prophecy of the Curse-Breaker and then we all fought
the wolves together?" I asked him.

"Yeah, I remember. What about it?" he said.

"Well. . . I saw the way you acted, back then. You used to
think it mattered to break the Curse; I know you did, even though
you never talked about it much. That day when you went down to
the deer camp all by yourself, I thought that was the bravest thing
I ever saw anybody do in my whole life. So, if there are still all
these pods out there, and especially if they're hurting people, then
don't you think we ought to finish what we started, or at least
try?" I asked him. That was stark truth, straight as an arrow, and
all I could do was pray that he'd listen.

He didn't answer me right away, though. He just looked out the
window where the sun was setting across Coca Cola Lake, and
played with the bullet on a string that he still wore around his
neck sometimes. When he spoke again, he sounded moody.

"I never wanted to fight wolves all my life, Zach. I want to go
skating, and play ball after school, and cruise State Line and
whistle at pretty girls, and hang out at the mall, and all that stuff
normal people do. I want. . . oh, I don't know. I want to get a
good job someday and fall in love and have three or four kids and
go to church every Sunday and live happily ever after. That's *all*
I want, Zach. I'm not like you. I don't want to be a crusader or a
dragon-slayer or whatever you want to call it. That's not who I
am," he said after a while.

It's not like Cameron to be that serious, or even to talk about
stuff like that at all, and I knew I must have hit a deep nerve.

"I know that, Cam, and I don't want to do it for always, either.
I want to end it this time for good and all, if we can find a way.
But I need your help, bubba; I can't do it by myself," I said.

He looked at me for a long time with that same scowl on his face, and I could almost watch him struggling inside between how much he loved me and how much he hated crusading.

"You know I'll help if I can," he finally said, although he still didn't sound very happy about it.

"Yeah, I know," I told him heavily. Maybe he knew he was making me feel bad, because he wiped the scowl off his face with an effort and gave me a crooked smile.

"All right, then, where do we start?" he asked.

The full version of
More Golden Than Day
is available now at your favorite retailer.

Author's Note

I wrote this book largely because of the many requests I received to hear more about Zach and his adventures, and to satisfy my own curiosity about him. Characters sometimes take on a life of their own, and authors are no more immune to that curiosity than anyone else is, even when we created the character ourselves.

While working on this book, I discovered that sequels are hard to write. It takes a lot of thought to connect the two stories into a seamless whole, and it also requires that you don't simply rehash what you said in the first book; there has to be something more and bigger. In *Cry for the Moon,* Zach had to deal with rejection and the pain of deciding to be true to what he thought was right. Those themes were continued in this story, but he also had to face new issues as well, such as how much faith he was willing to put in God and how much compassion he would have for others. In *Behind Blue Eyes,* Zach grew a little stronger and a little closer to becoming the kind of man I hope he will be someday. I see him deepening his relationship with God, with his family, and with all the things that he holds dear, and I find that I actually like the kid and wish he were here to talk to now and then. I think I might learn a lot from someone like him.

There will be at least one more book about Zach, since I would like very much to finish watching him grow up.

The title, *Behind Blue Eyes,* has several meanings. The obvious one, of course, is that the story is largely about the inner thoughts and feelings of Zach and Cameron, who are cousins with the same unusually blue eyes which are the mark of the curse-breaker. The allusion to the song of the same name (which is briefly discussed in the story) is another.

Readers will notice that Zach's mood is a little more grown-up in this book than it was in *Cry for the Moon.* That's intentional. There's a lot of growing and developing that gets done between twelve and fourteen, and Zach isn't quite the same kid he used to be, although his personality is still very recognizable, I think.

I hope readers who loved and enjoyed Zach's earlier adventures will enjoy these just as much. I know I did.

William Woodall
July 21, 2010

Discussion Questions

1. Zach finds himself in a completely unexpected situation when he is kidnapped from his back yard, yet he manages to keep a cool head and think quickly. How do you think you might react, if something similar happened to you?

2. When he overhears Cameron getting slapped, Zach decides to see if he can help him escape also, even though they are complete strangers at the time. How would you have felt in this situation if you were Zach? Would you have handled the situation any differently?

3. Cameron is fourteen years old, and yet he hasn't become a *loup-garou* yet. Why do you think the wolves haven't cursed him yet?

4. When it begins to seem that Cameron might come to live with them permanently, Zach finds that he has mixed feelings about that idea, and even some jealousy. How would you feel if you suddenly had a new brother or sister you didn't expect?

5. Many times, Zach struggles with the thought of whether he should trust God in difficult circumstances. Have there ever been times when you have had to trust God even though it wasn't easy? Talk about those times, or imagine a time when you might have to face that kind of situation.

6. Justin says that sometimes we have responsibilities even when we didn't choose them or didn't want them. Do you agree with that idea? Explain why or why not.

7. Zach says that we conquer through love, or not at all. Explain what you think he meant by that idea.

8. When Zach reads the story of Joram Ross, he is inspired to think that he could do something similar. Has there ever been a time when a story you read or a person you knew inspired you in some way?

9. In Longview, Zach says that Justin gave him courage when he was scared to do what needed to be done. Have you ever had to do something that was scary? Talk about that time, and explain who or what you think helped you to overcome your fear.

10. Zach uses the last of the water to save Cameron's life in Lebanon, even though he thinks this will mean giving up on his plan to destroy the wolf-stones. Would you have made the same choice, or would you

have taken the chance on making it to the hospital in time? Explain your thinking.

11. The werewolves seem willing to fight tooth and nail to preserve their stones and their Curse. Why do you think they are so determined to preserve these things?

12. There are no records of what happened to Daniel Trewick after he suddenly stopped writing in his journal. What do you think might have happened to him?

13. Justin says that one of the reasons he loves Eileen is because her heart is even more beautiful than her face. Explain what you think he meant.

14. Zach says that at the heart of darkness, there's always a nugget of gold. Explain what you think this means. Do you agree or disagree with this idea?

15. While reading the journal, Zach says that he always hoped his family members would turn out to be people who were good and brave and who loved God. The fact that they were *not* that kind of people was a crushing disappointment to him. Has there ever been a time when someone you admired let you down? If so, how did that affect the way you felt about that person?

16. Zach says that every choice we make and everything we do (or don't do) has consequences, sometimes highly unexpected ones. Has there ever been a time when you did something that had unforeseen results later on? Discuss that experience, and whether the results were good or bad ones.

17. Other than Zach himself, who was your favorite character from this book? Discuss why you liked this person so well.

The Curse-Breaker Books
By *William Woodall*

Long ago, there was a Godly woman named Marybeth Trewick, who for various reasons found herself married to a rich but wicked man named Daniel who practiced all kinds of evil. She could only watch helplessly as her five sons grew up to become just as wicked as their father, and as her only daughter was forced to flee for her life lest she be killed.

But in the midst of her despair, God sent Marybeth a dream that after seven generations had passed, there would be five boys born to replace and redeem the ones that she had lost. These five would be breakers of curses and fighters against all things wicked and evil, and each of them would have the same vividly blue eyes, the same color as Marybeth's.

And even though the Curse-Breakers are each called to very different tasks in the world, the basic goal of fighting evil and loving God is always the same. These are their names and stories.

Brian Stone: The oldest curse-breaker, Brian's task is to save his brother's life and to remind men of Heaven by showing them the beauty of what could have been if the world had never fallen.

Cody McGrath: Two years younger than Brian, Cody is called to break the power of a dangerous sorceress. He's a dreamer of true dreams and a healer of the lost and broken-hearted.

Zachary Trewick: Four years younger than Cody, Zach is called to destroy one of the worst remaining aspects of his ancestor's wickedness; the werewolf curse which most of his family still embrace wholeheartedly.

Cameron Parker: Cameron and Zach are the same age, not to mention third cousins and best friends. Cameron has a big role to play in the struggle against the wolves, and later becomes the leader of all the survivors of Earth.

Brandon Stone: Brian's little brother, Brandon is three years younger than Cameron and Zach. He has a gift to know the meaning of dreams, and he is called to defend the weak and to uphold all that is righteous and true.

The Curse-Breaker Books form a collection of related stories about these five boys and sometimes their children. Each series tells the tale of a different Curse-Breaker (or sometimes more than one), but they also fit together in ways you wouldn't expect, in order to form a single unified storyline. It's helpful to read the books in order if possible, but it's not strictly necessary. You can read more about each series on the following pages.

The Last Werewolf Hunter Series
By William Woodall

Zach Trewick always thought he'd become a writer someday, or maybe play baseball for the Texas Rangers. What he never imagined in his craziest dreams was that he'd find himself dodging bullets and crashing cars off mountainsides, let alone that he'd ever be expected to break the ancient werewolf curse which hangs over his family.

But Zach is the last of the werewolf hunters, the long-foretold Curse-Breaker who can wipe out the wolves forever, and he's not the type to give up just because of a few minor setbacks. . .

Cry for the Moon: What would you do, if your family wanted you to become a monster? What if they wouldn't take no for an answer? When 12 year old Zach faces questions like these, he seems to have only one choice; *run.* Thus begins a long search for refuge, and perhaps redemption also.

Behind Blue Eyes: When a stranger kidnaps him from his own back yard, Zach soon finds that the past isn't quite as dead as he might wish. For the time has come at last for Zach and his cousin Cameron to break the wolf curse forever; and his family has no intention of letting that happen.

More Golden Than Day: When his girlfriend Jolie and then Cameron fall into the hands of the wolves, Zach has no choice but to take on his enemies for a second round. Only this time the stakes are horribly high, and if he fails he may end up losing everything he's ever loved.

Truesilver: When a family of wicked ex-wolves is accidentally awakened, Zach soon finds himself locked in a desperate fight for survival that he never anticipated. And even though he's sworn an oath to fight evil to the utmost of his power, there are times when courage is awfully hard to come by.

* * * * * * *

"If you are looking for a story about a boy who learns valuable lessons about family, love, friendship and God this is the book for you. I recommend this book to a pre-teen or adult. I truly enjoyed this book."
-Rae, *My Book Addiction Reviews*

"I found myself captivated with the story and could not stop reading until I reached the final page. Everything about this story is thought-provoking. Readers of all ages will appreciate this wonderfully told story,"
-Jancy, Kansas

The Stones of Song Series
By William Woodall

"There's a thing called magnanimity, or greatness of heart, and to me it's the most beautiful thing that ever there was. It means courage, but it's more than that. It means to cast aside all thought of yourself for the sake of another, like Moses in Gilead or the martyrs who died with a smile on their face. In its own small way it's a reflection of the Lord Jesus at Calvary, and therefore of God, the Light so beautiful that no one who sees it can ever turn away."

So says Cody McGrath, and in many ways that statement is the central theme of this series; the casting away of self for love of another, the scorning of selfishness in all its forms.

These are the stories of the Stone family: Brian, Jenny, Lisa, and Brandon, and some of the people they know and love, most notably Cody. All of them were called for great and glorious things, though sometimes only after great suffering and many mistakes.

<u>Unclouded Day:</u> Brian Stone's life isn't easy. Abandoned by his father, abused by his alcoholic mother, and mocked by his classmates, his only treasures are his beloved little brother and his old guitar. This is the tale of his journey to find the Fountain of Youth, and perhaps to save the world.

<u>Many Waters:</u> Lisa Stone is a small-town waitress with heavy burdens to bear. Cody is a young cowboy with mystical dreams and some very dangerous enemies. But when the two of them must face down an evil witch who tries to destroy their very lives, it seems only a miracle can save them.

<u>Bran the Blessed:</u> Brandon Stone hasn't always made the right choices in life, but he's never found himself in quite such deep trouble as this. But even though his life seems ruined forever, Bran still has a high calling to answer. . . if he can find the courage.

* * * * * * *

"I would absolutely, without reservation, encourage you to read this wonderful novel, even if you aren't the fantasy genre type. It was a blessing."
-Sue, *Reflections and Reviews*

"There are so many nuggets of truth in this book. It's about Heaven. It's about bad things happening for a reason. It's about deciding for yourself what truly matters most in life. It's a really good book!"
-Tattie, *Christian Fiction Ebooks*

The Tyke McGrath Series
By *William Woodall*

In the year 2154, the world has become a dangerous place. Extremist groups would like nothing better than to wipe out humanity completely, and even the people sworn to defend civilization against such threats have become deeply corrupt and untrustworthy.

When a virulent plague destroys all warm-blooded life on Earth, a small band of survivors clings to life on the partially-terraformed Moon. But fresh dangers lie in wait for the unwary; nor have they left behind all the wickedness in the hearts of men.

Nightfall: When Micah McGrath suddenly finds himself thrust into a dangerous and ugly future after a lab accident, his only choice is to make the best life for himself that he can. But when the secret police get wind of his research into time travel, he soon finds himself in deep trouble indeed.

Tycho: Tycho McGrath is a high school honor student in Florida when he discovers a terrifying secret: a man-made bacterium is about to wipe out all warm-blooded life on Earth within days. The only hope for survival is to flee at once, a plan which carries its own set of unexpected dangers.

Avenger: After spotting an SOS coming from the abandoned Moon, the survivors must organize a rescue mission. But the expedition quickly becomes far more complicated, leading them to the icy world of Titan in search of a holy mountain that no human eye has ever seen.

Freedom: When a cruel and power-hungry military commander on Venus decides to reconquer Earth, the only thing he needs is the formula for Tyke's Orion vaccine. The survivors soon find themselves locked into a bitter battle over the future of mankind, and who will inherit the Earth after all.

Elysium: What began as a simple mission to recover lost comrades in the Martian desert quickly turns deadly when Tyke and the others find *themselves* stranded on the Red Planet, with only the slimmest of chances to make it home again, or to fulfill the destiny which God has in store for them.

* * * * * * *

"Reminiscent of Freedom's Landing, by Anne McCaffrey, Tycho combines the best of traditional space-exploration sci-fi with modern apocalyptic fiction. For any fans of hard science fiction, it doesn't get much better than this."

- Liz, OH2 Reviews

Trewick Family Tree

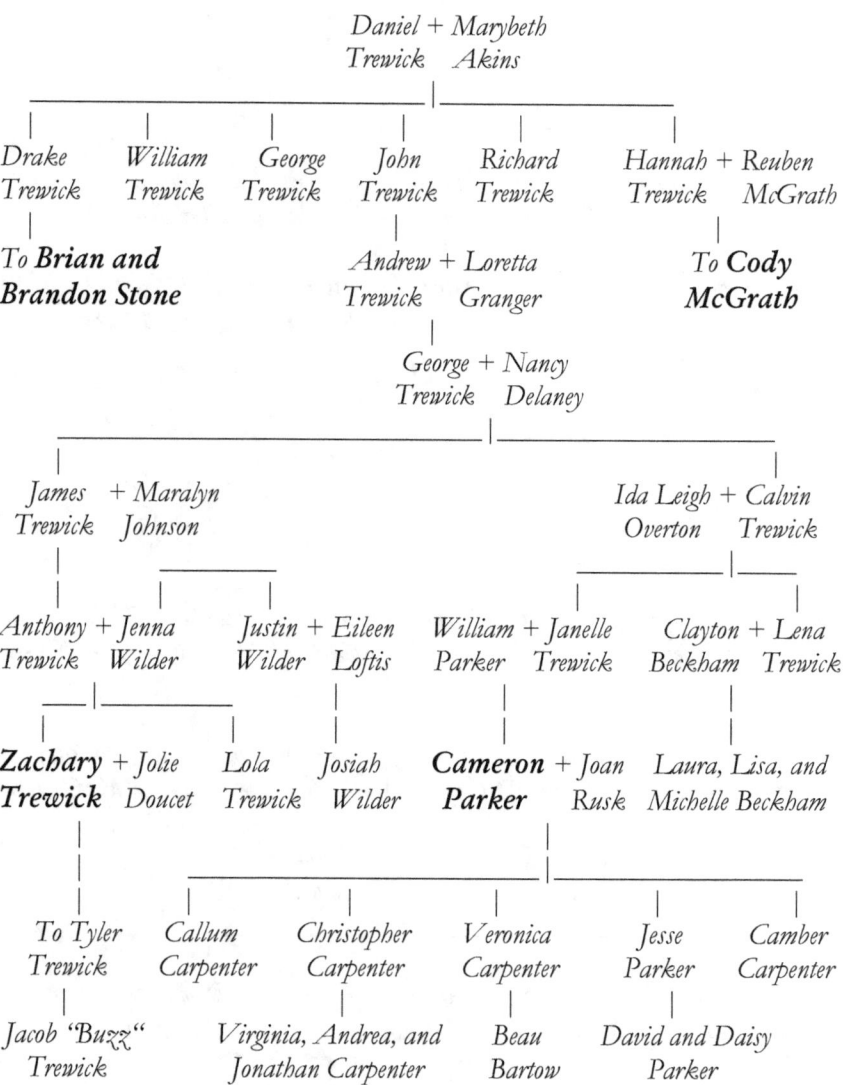

Daniel + Marybeth
Trewick   Akins

Drake Trewick | William Trewick | George Trewick | John Trewick | Richard Trewick | Hannah + Reuben
Trewick   McGrath

To **Brian and Brandon Stone**

Andrew + Loretta
Trewick   Granger

To **Cody McGrath**

George + Nancy
Trewick   Delaney

James + Maralyn
Trewick   Johnson

Ida Leigh + Calvin
Overton   Trewick

Anthony + Jenna
Trewick   Wilder

Justin + Eileen
Wilder   Loftis

William + Janelle
Parker   Trewick

Clayton + Lena
Beckham   Trewick

Zachary + Jolie
Trewick   Doucet

Lola Trewick

Josiah Wilder

Cameron + Joan
Parker   Rusk

Laura, Lisa, and
Michelle Beckham

To Tyler Trewick

Callum Carpenter

Christopher Carpenter

Veronica Carpenter

Jesse Parker

Camber Carpenter

Jacob "Buzz" Trewick

Virginia, Andrea, and
Jonathan Carpenter

Beau Bartow

David and Daisy
Parker

1. Curse-Breakers are in bold.
2. Cameron Parker later changed his name to Philip Carpenter.
3. Tyler Trewick is Zach's great-grandson.
4. Lisa Beckham's husband is Logan Tygart.
5. Laura Beckham's husband is Heath Coates, son of Albert Coates.
6. More complete family trees are available on the author's website.

Trewick Family Tree

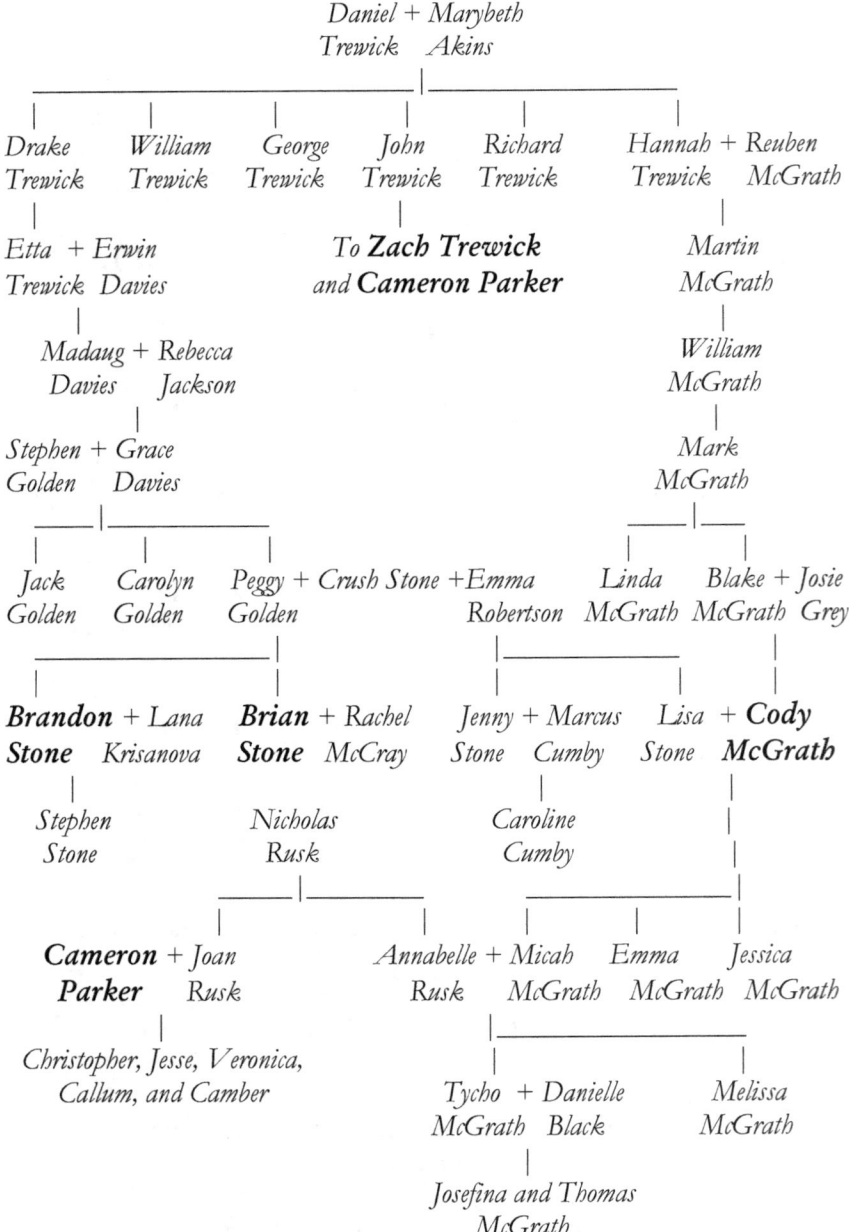

Doucet Family Tree

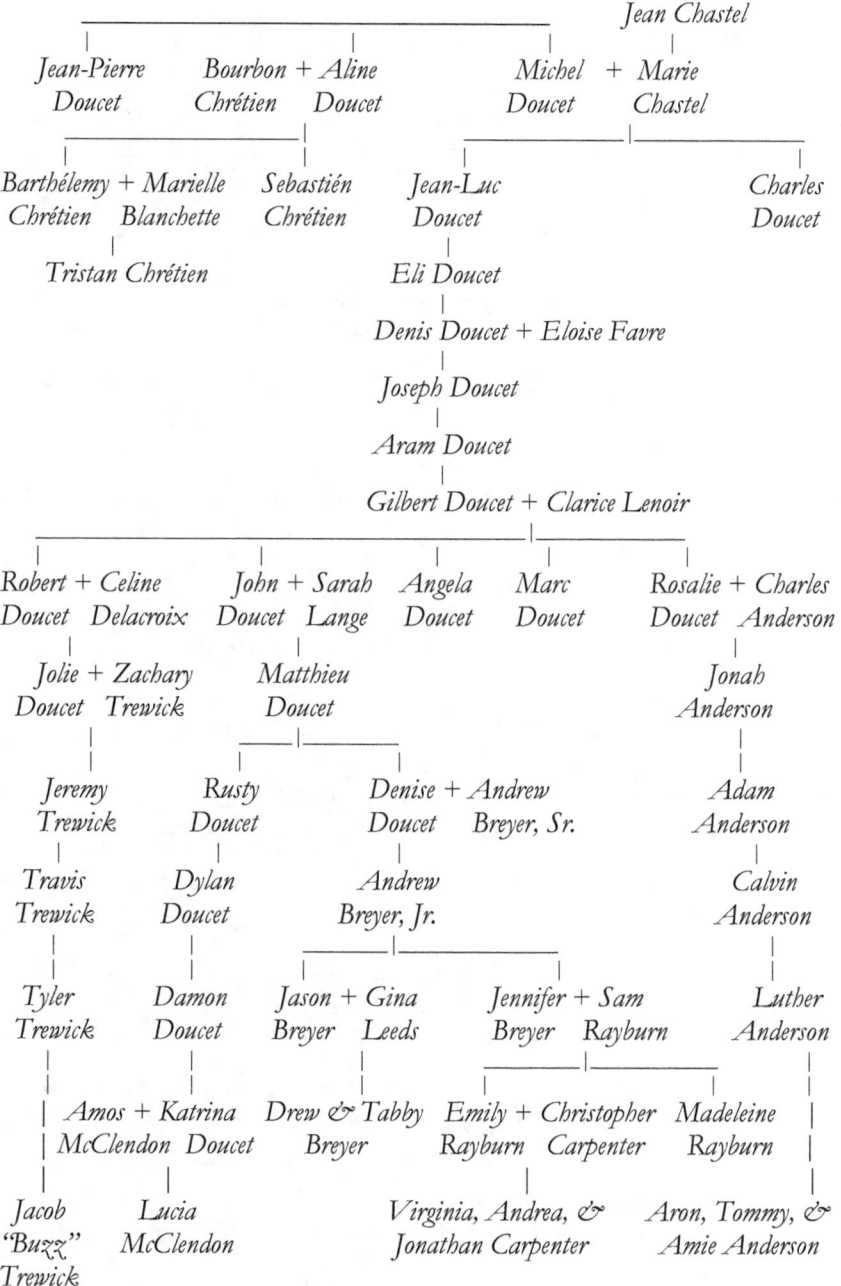

Bartow Family Tree

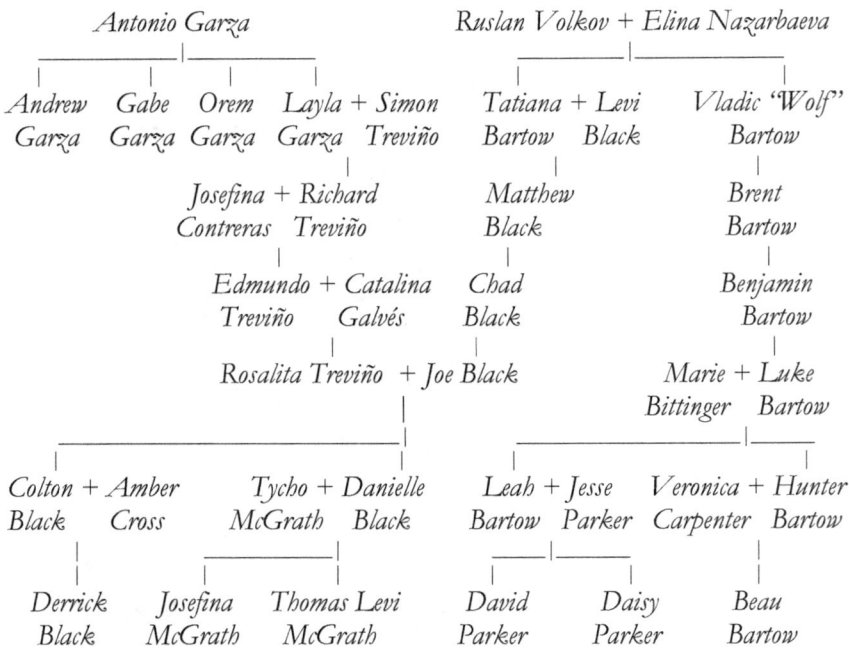

Jones and Golden Family Trees

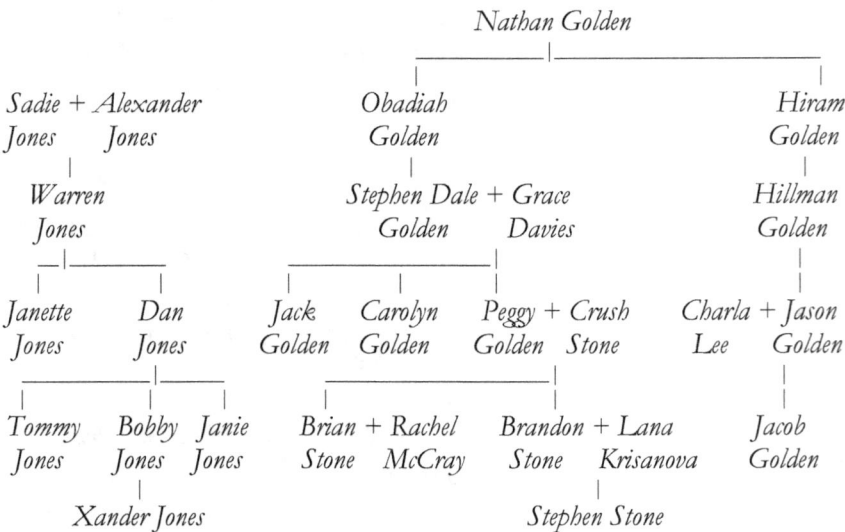

*If you'd like to find out more about
these and other books,
please visit:*

**William Woodall's
Official Author Website**

www.williamwoodall.org

Here you will find:

Free short stories

Discussion questions for teachers and book clubs

Free sample chapters of all my books

Photos of characters and locations for each story

Articles

Interviews

Quotable Quotes

Contact Information

And much, much more!

www.ingramcontent.com/pod-product-compliance
Lightning Source LLC
Chambersburg PA
CBHW050931120626
46552CB00001B/151